J. H. (Joseph Henry) Shorthouse

The Countess Eve

J. H. (Joseph Henry) Shorthouse

The Countess Eve

ISBN/EAN: 9783337414368

Printed in Europe, USA, Canada, Australia, Japan

Cover: Foto ©Andreas Hilbeck / pixelio.de

More available books at **www.hansebooks.com**

THE

COUNTESS EVE

BY

J. H. SHORTHOUSE

AUTHOR OF 'JOHN INGLESANT,' 'SIR PERCIVAL, THE LITTLE
SCHOOLMASTER MARK, ETC

London

MACMILLAN AND CO.

AND NEW YORK

1888

That it may please Thee to strengthen such as do stand, and to comfort and help the weak-hearted, and to raise up them that fall, and finally to beat down Satan under our feet.

THE COUNTESS EVE

I

In the science of sound there are partial tones, which are unheard, but which blend with the tones that are heard, and make all the difference between the paltry note of the poorest instrument and the supreme note of a violin. So, in the science of life, in the crowded street or market-place or theatre, or wherever life is, there are partial tones, there are unseen presences. Side by side with the human crowd is a crowd of unseen forms—Principalities and

Œ B

Powers and Possibilities. These are unseen, but not unfelt. They enter into the
houses of the human beings that are seen,
and for their coming some of them are
swept and garnished, and they abide there,
and the last state of these human beings
is radiant with a divine light and resonant
with an added tone; or, on the contrary,
it may be that, haunted by spirits more
wicked than themselves, the last state of
such beings is worse than before—subject
to a violence and tyranny abhorrent even
to themselves; impalpable and inevitable,
as it would seem, even to the confines of
despair. In the quaint streets of an old
French provincial city, as in the proudest
cities of the world, something like this was
happening, and not in this city only, or at

the time we write of, or to the few people we are trying to know something about, but to all people, and in all places, and during every day and through every night, as long as human life shall endure.

In the year 1785, or thereabouts, the events which are about to be related are said to have occurred in a city of Burgundy which shall be nameless. It is not of much consequence whether these events occurred in Chalons, or Dijon, or Besançon, or Dole, but it does seem to me important for the understanding of the story that the reader should form in his mind some image of the old high-roofed, gabled and walled city, mellowed and crumbling with age, standing amidst meadows and orchards and vineyards

upon the sunny slopes, and the winding
river and millpools, and, beyond, the
gradual rise of woodland toward the Jura
mountains, with their fir forests and deep
valleys and sudden rain-storms, and the
white cliffs shining against the delicate
southern sky.

Outside the city, a lovely *paysage*,
picturesque with uncultivated lands, with
wretched peasants herded into a few
miserable villages, with numberless poor
nobles prouder than they were poor,
living in farmhouses and ruinous small
châteaux, with here and there the great
isolated château of a *grand seigneur*, an
absentee and a courtier in Paris.

Inside the city, narrow, winding streets
with rough, stone pavements, and gutters

down their midst, lofty gabled houses, and
wharves and *halles* by the river. A
swarm of *notables* and privileged middle
classes, paying no taxes, hated by the un-
privileged, taxed, down-trodden people.
A small class, half noble, half *bourgeois*,
who preferred the city to the country.
A society perfectly provincial, with no
thought, with no hope, beyond its narrow
horizon—a society frivolous, petty, plea-
sure-seeking, pleased with infinitely small
pleasures ; dancing, laughing, chattering
from day to day.

In the city, as in all French cities, was
a theatre, in this case one of higher character than was common, and at the time this
story commences it was occupied by a
company of players of more than ordinary

capacity, who were performing with distinguished success, and attracting the
gentry and populace of the city and province to their acting and singing.

Among the members of this company
were two young men, one of them an
actor, the other a musician. The actor,
who was slightly the elder of the two and
was named Felix la Valliere, was the
descendant of a family of actors of the
school of Molière; the other, Claude de
Brie, was the offspring of a family of
penniless nobles, whose father had married
a girl as penniless as himself. As he
had stolen this girl away from her convent school, and had by such conduct
broken through all the *convenances* of
his order, and alienated himself from his

family, he was cut off from the only
resource of the boys of penniless noble
families—the marine. He renounced by
his own act—doubtless very fortunately
for himself—the life of aimless, listless
inactivity entailed on many of his order,
and struck out a new path and re-
sorted to acting and to music for a liveli-
hood.   His son followed the latter
profession.

These two young men, whose fathers
had been intimate friends, were insepar-
able companions. Of the most opposite
temperaments, the very difference of their
characters seemed only to cement their
friendship.

They were both handsome, but of very
different styles.   La Valliere, the actor,

was slight and elegant in build, with a changeful, facile expression of feature and of attitude, singularly attractive and fascinating. His friend, to a figure noble and distinguished, added an expression of perfect sweetness combined with steadiness and gravity. They were, doubtless, a striking pair.

As an actor la Valliere was at once the darling and the perplexity of the manager of his company and of his fellows, many of whom indeed considered him to be nothing less than a madman. He was so popular that his eccentricities were overlooked, and his violation of all law condoned. He so entirely associated himself with the characters he represented on the stage, that he lost himself

in them, or rather they were lost in him,
and consequently he scarcely ever acted a
part in the same way for long together,
suddenly changing his conception and
interpretation of the character as the
whim or fancy of the moment prompted
him. This was less objectionable in those
days, when the same piece was rarely
given on two consecutive nights, than it
would be at the present day ; but it will
easily be seen that such a tendency would
be perplexing to his companions.

What is still more important, however,
is that what la Valliere was on the stage
he was also in real life. He regarded
life and all mankind as only the shifting
scenes and persons of a stage play. What
he did himself he was willing to allow of

or to expect in others, so that no settled conduct or regular law of action was to be expected of society so far as he was concerned; and not only was moral law unknown, as it seemed, to him, but physical law seemed also uncertain and insecure, so that nothing that could have happened in the world of sense would have surprised him, and he was an avowed believer in Mesmer and the fashionable cabalistic *diablerie* of the day. It is possible that the lack of physical certainty explained the want of moral firmness, for if a man is not sure of the ground under his feet, he is not likely, as men go, to be more certain of the heaven over his head.

As on the stage he could not properly be said to *act*, for he played every part simply as it presented itself to his own fancy, so in life he could scarcely be considered a responsible or moral being, so completely did the dramatic impulse of the moment, or of the situation, carry him with it.

In surprising contrast to this gay and lawless creature was his bosom friend, Claude de Bric, one of those rare natures to whom God has given the faculty of purity, and training has given the winsome grace of an ideal life.

. . . . .

The play was over, and the two friends came out by a side door into the wet street. Muffled in their long cloaks, and picking their way as they best could through the mire and over the huge stones of the causeway, by the light of a chance lantern or of a still open shop, they were startled by the passing of a large carriage accompanied by servants, and the next moment by its sudden halt. ˙Over the house-tops a bright moon, shining out from between the dark rain clouds, lent a sudden lustre to the murky by-street.

'Sir,' said a servant, who had descended from the box-seat of the carriage, 'if, as I believe, you are Monsieur Felix la Valliere, Monsieur le Comte du Pic-Adam requests the honour of your company at supper at his château without the Gate de Veaux.'

'I am most honoured by the invitation of Monsieur le Comte,' replied la Valliere, 'but I have with me my friend Monsieur de Brie, who is spending the evening with me.'

'Sir,' replied the servant with lofty politeness, ' I am quite sure that Monsieur le Comte would not wish to separate you from your friend. Monsieur le Comte will be honoured by the company of you both.'

He turned back towards the carriage with an air which said plainly—

'When *we* choose to condescend we are not the people to do things by halves.'

'Fortune favours us,' whispered la Valliere to his friend. ' This is that old diplomatist who has married the lovely young wife whom they call the Countess Eve.'

Picking their way as well as might be across the muddy street, the two young men approached the carriage, which stood surrounded by servants carrying links.

As they reached the carriage they were greeted from within by a bland and courteous personage, apparently of middle age, but who might be younger than he looked —a lofty, distinguished man, with a distrait and absent expression, but scrupulously polite.

'Sir,' he said, 'it is most kind of you to respond to my unceremonious invitation, and to bring your friend with you. The Countess has been much gratified by your acting to-night. Pray enter the carriage. The Countess du Pic-Adam.'

The young men entered the carriage and placed themselves on the front seat, opposite to the Count and Countess.

By the light of the flambeaux the Count
certainly seemed younger than he had at
first appeared. He had a fair steadfast
countenance, and a suave, bland manner
and tone. He seemed to de Brie, who
was a student of character, to be descended
from a mixed ancestry.

'Madame la Comtesse,' he said, 'has
been so delighted with your acting to-
night, Monsieur la Valliere, that she wished
to be acquainted more closely with one
who has given her so much pleasure.'

By the light of the torches a lovely
face, buried in masses of white fur, looked
out from the corner of the carriage upon
the two young men, and a melodious voice
said—

'Monsieur de Brie, I believe, is the

performer of that lovely obbligato to Mademoiselle Mori's song.'

'Madame la Comtesse is perfectly right,' said la Valliere eagerly, 'and my friend has his violin with him, so that if after supper Madame would like to hear the air again?'——

The uneasy motion of the carriage over the rough pavement prevented much conversation, but the distance to the city gate was short, and after they had passed the drawbridge and the glacis the road was easier, and a few minutes afterwards the carriage turned into an avenue lighted by the fitful moonbeams, which traversed a small park leading to a modern château. Numerous servants received the Count and his lady in the great hall, and the two young men were conducted to a private room where they might to some extent make themselves ready for supper.

The supper-table was spread before a large and noble fireplace of carved stone reaching almost to the roof of a large *salle*. Screens of Chinese work sheltered the party, and beyond them stretched the dark and limitless shadows of an unknown and mysterious world. The Countess had changed her dress, and came to the supper-table in a robe of white satin, with strings of pearls in her hair. She had rich chestnut hair and deep violet eyes. The young men thought her the most mysteriously lovely creature they had ever seen.

The supper was delicate and delicious, and the Burgundy of the choicest growth.

The conversation turned naturally upon art and the stage, and la Valliere, warmed with the generous wine, became eloquent on this theme.

'I can conceive nothing more delight- ful,' said the Countess, 'than this art, which gives you the power of pleasing others simply by the exertion of a faculty the exertion of which must be such a delight to yourself. I can think of nothing more attractive than the power of representing, at your own choice, Nature in all her vagaries—of treating at will all the diverse paths of life—of the following in your own person all the fortunes, all the vicissitudes, all the hopes and conceptions of a man. The world seems to me to be at your feet. You live every kind of life at will.'

'That is the ideal actor,' said la Valliere, 'not at all the commonplace one. I have often been amused to see an old man—not a bad actor either—go through all the little tricks of action and tone of voice which he had practised for thirty years, because he had been taught so long ago that these were the correct adjuncts of the part, and never once during the whole of that time living in, realising, the part himself. For myself, I seem to live a different life each night. I seldom act even the same part precisely in the same way twice together. I seem to see fresh meanings and purposes in my part. Fresh complications occur, fresh incidents suggest themselves. I am born again every night.'

'It is an inconvenient practice on the part of an actor,' said de Brie, smiling; 'my friend has been much blamed for it.'

'Art,' said la Valliere, 'must never be crippled or confined. Indeed, all life must be free and untrammelled, or it is not life. He who would be really a man must know all that the life of man can be, must be free to choose and to enjoy, free to test his powers in all directions, to taste of all the enjoyments and faculties at his disposal; to probe to the uttermost the possibilities not only of the seen but of the unseen existence; to feel and to enjoy to the very full all that Nature possesses, or that man can dream, of life and thought. Give me the man who acts on the impulse of his nature—not upon a balanced, *bourgeois*

consideration of what is due to his class, or
his character, or his principles.'

'You have not, Monsieur la Valliere,'
said the Count, looking very fixedly at
Felix, and speaking very slowly, 'you
have not, I venture to think, put all this
theory of life into practice, except upon
the stage.   Otherwise, I hardly think
that you would speak as cheerfully as
you do.'

His tone was so solemn, and his manner so marked, that the two young men
looked at him with some surprise.

The Countess also raised her eyes, and
it seemed to Claude de Brie, who watched
her closely, that a little shudder passed
over her exquisite form, and that her eyes
were turned furtively in the direction of

her husband, with a lingering, hopeless
look.

There was a short but awkward pause.
La Valliere seemed for the moment unaccountably silenced, but before de Brie
could recover himself sufficiently to speak,
the Count seemed to make an effort, and,
as though conscious of his duty as host,
continued in a gayer tone.

'This talk is too grave for a supper
after the play. You cannot possibly, gentlemen, return to the city to-night. The
gates will not open even to my carriages.
My people will, I hope, find you all things
necessary, and I should like you to see
our gardens in the morning light. The
private garden is considered by some to
be very quaint and well laid out. We call

it'—and the Count looked kindly, and
even tenderly, across the table at his
young wife—'we call it Paradise.'

The Countess's face flushed with a kind
of delighted surprise, but it relapsed again
in a moment into its usual listless, hopeless
expression, as the kindly glance faded as
rapidly from her husband's eyes.

'Paradise,' said la Valliere, speaking
apparently to the great branched candelabra before him, 'Paradise.   That was
what I was meaning when I spoke of the
possibilities of existence, whether seen or
unseen.   I did not know that it was so
near.'

As he spoke a servant from behind his
chair filled up his glass with the luscious
Burgundy.

'Felix,' said his friend across the table, in a soft, quiet voice, but with no affectation of an aside, 'do not drink any more wine. You have had enough.'

The actor looked for a moment across the table into his friend's eyes. Then he put his glass back from him and rose quietly from his seat.

'I promised Madame,' he said, 'that she should hear the air on the violin. If one of the servants would bring the instrument from the hall this might be a suitable moment.'

'It is only the obbligato that Madame can hear,' said de Brie. 'We shall not have Mademoiselle Mori's lovely notes; but in all beautiful compositions of sound, or colour, or form, there is, just so far as they are pure and perfect, a unity and a beauty of which no part can exist selfishly or apart from the rest. So that, in the simple air as drawn from the strings, it is possible that Madame may recognise something of the old fascination. Let us hope that she may.'

'I engage that she will,' la Valliere broke in eagerly; 'it is the prerogative of all things in Nature—all things lovely, true and ideal—to act harmoniously together. Madame la Comtesse'—he seemed again to be addressing the candelabra—'cannot escape from this necessity, for it is a condition of the highest loveliness—even of her own.'

De Brie's advice had evidently not been given too soon.

While he spoke, as if to cover his last words, la Valliere had risen and drawn back his chair from the table and had placed it by the side of the lofty, carved fireplace, and the Count withdrew his chair from the end of the table to a position not far from him ; the Countess moved from her seat to a settee sheltered by one of the large screens, and de Brie, coming round the table, stood leaning against it in front of the fire, his violin in his hand.

La Valliere had taken just enough wine to excite his fancy, and to produce that sensation of expectancy under which the strangest things may happen without exciting surprise. He sat back quietly in his chair, a sense of restraint and caution upon him, his head leaning against the carved stone pilaster of the mantel-piece, and de Brie began to play.

A plaintive, continuous note, searching back into a past eternity, stretching forward into all time, stirred his senses into activity, and la Valliere looked across to where the Countess sat.

She lay back upon the cushioned settee, her sad eyes fixed upon the dancing fire-light, with no expression in them but that of a resigned weariness—of a hopeless consciousness of mistake, of a mistaken effort and of an aim that had failed—a resigned weariness that roused itself every now and then to look up with a momentary hope into her husband's face, as with a longing for some interest in life and in him, only to fall back again before his polished, stony, absent air.

Behind her the fantastic forms of strange birds and flowers on the great Chinese screen shut out the shadowy distance of the vast *salon*, and before her hovered restlessly the plumed whiteness of a great fan that lay, rather than was held, in her listless hands.

The plaintive note changed into the clear, holy joy of a pure love that meets its fellow and is glad, and la Vallierc's eyes gleamed with a sudden terror indescribable in words, for from behind the gay, flowering screen, out of the weird darkness beyond, there glided a faint, shadowy figure and stood beside the Countess's couch, leaning towards her

as if to speak. Faint and almost indefinite
at first, the figure became momentarily
more distinct. A strange, absorbing feeling took possession of la Valliere's mind
—in answer, as it seemed, to a correspond-
ing effort on the part of the appearance
itself—an intense desire for a clearer
vision; for though the figure apparently
concentrated its attention entirely upon
the Countess, yet there emanated from
it, so to speak, an indescribable effluence
of temptation and attraction, luring la
Valliere's fancy to endeavour to see more
clearly, to be better acquainted with what
he saw.

As the bewitching strains of the violin
continued, and this mysterious intruder
became more clear and distinct to his

excited sense, it seemed to la Valliere
that a figure, habited as a French abbé,
was leaning on the arm of the Countess's seat and whispering in her ear.
It seemed that its presence was unper-
ceived by the Countess herself, or by any
of the other persons in the room; but
after a few seconds of this strange intercourse—if such it could be called—the attitude and manner of the Countess changed
inexplicably. She raised her eyes from
the fire, and her look had undergone a
surprising change. The hopeless weariness was gone, and in its place was an
expression of startled, expectant interest
and excitement, subdued and chastened,
but real and strong. Did la Valliere
deceive himself, or, in the soft, dreamy

light across the tremulous motion of the
fan, was this altered look directed towards
himself? Did it say?—certainly he inter-
preted it so to say—'In place of stony
indifference, of cold abstraction and repug-
nance almost, shall I not find, can I not
find, the love for which I yearn—the sympathy and tenderness—elsewhere? And
if elsewhere, surely here.'

The glamour of a dream seemed to
pervade the whole scene—the softened
light, the leaping flame of the wood fire,
the strains of the violin—and over all a
sense of mystic atmosphere, within which
all things seemed transfigured, a thin
golden haze of soft light, in which la
Valliere's face and slight figure became
more attractive and the loveliness of the

Countess more lovely still; and always, in la Valliere's eyes, the figure by the couch became clearer and more clear, till at last it turned its face directly towards the young man, and the eyes met his with a quite friendly, confidential gaze.

It was certainly the figure of a French abbé, but the expression of the face was such as no French abbé—no, nor any other man—had ever displayed. For the moment it was that of an almost amiable suavity—almost, because the peculiarity of the face consisted in the conviction that the sight of it produced, that any expression it might wear was only for a moment; that any amiable or pleasing expression especially was but the result of effort, the mere masque of an actor, not the result of amiability itself.

It was an expression instinct with a sense of change, infinitely fugitive, protean, indicating nothing, it. seemed, so much as an indefinite capacity, which, in whatever direction it might tend, was certainly not suggestive of good.

This sense of change extended even to the features, so that no man could have positively defined them even to himself, much less have conveyed any idea of them to others. The most that could be said of them was, that they conveyed a general impression of power and of a certain distinction; not exactly, however, in the sense in which men generally understand the word, for it seemed to arise from the fact that the origin was indefinite and immaterial

D

rather than as springing from matter or as born of race.

The friendly gaze, if it were friendly, penetrated into la Valliere's nature as no human gaze had ever done before. Every thought of his heart, to the very depths of his being, seemed familiar to this strange influence and responsive to its call. Every tendency and facility which human frailty uses or suggests, every leaning of human life to the side of enjoyment, seemed to awake and to respond.

‘ Be bold,’ it seemed to say. ‘ Carry out your own theory of life. Enjoy, prove all things. Test the powers that have been given you, doubtless for use, by a beneficent Providence. Above all things be bold !’

La Valliere was not frightened. There was not even any feeling of wonder or of surprise connected with the appearance of this figure. What was produced was merely a sense of added power and a fresh life in every faculty and desire, of supreme luxury in the quickened perception of the shadowy room, of the glowing fire, of the dulcet music, above all of that lovely face and figure leaning forward from the large settee, with its background of fantastic screen, and the wonderful, entrancing look of the violet eyes. The strange, intruding figure with its intense individuality, seemed to shrink into the background and to wish to be forgotten. Perhaps its work was done.

The music ceased, and the Countess,

with a look of wearied falling back upon a disappointing present, arose and, thanking Claude de Brie politely, left the room. The Count summoned some domestics, and was on the point of consigning the two young men to their care, when la Valliere, inspired by a sudden impulse, spoke to him.

' Monsieur le Comte,' he said, ' I should have thought that your excellent Burgundy had turned my head, but that the appearance was so persistent and distinct. Monsieur l'Abbé, I presume—the ecclesiastic who was leaning on Madame's couch a moment ago, I could wish to have seen more of him—is probably not too desirous of making the acquaintance of strangers.'

He spoke, scarcely knowing what he said; the Burgundy had perhaps been more potent than he knew.

Something in his words, or in his tone, seemed to strike the Count as, with the echo of some familiar thought, he looked the young man straight in the eyes.

'Monsieur l'Abbé,' he said, 'the *directeur* of Madame la Comtesse, is at present from home on a visit *à ses terres*. I do not know who you may have seen. I saw no one but ourselves. But there are other beings than ourselves constantly around us—the remembrance of other days, the effects of past actions, the consequences of past sins, the trail, taint, poison of committed sin. Some we know and see, some we never see; they are perhaps the more fatal. You spoke of a man, had you told me that you had seen *her !*'—

La Valliere gazed at him with surprise.

'She must be always near me,' the Count went on, as if speaking to himself; 'always near me, and yet I never see her —never see her. May God, in His unspeakable pity, have mercy on me when I do.'

THE young men were shown into a lofty room in which were two beds and other luxurious furniture. Dark hangings of flowered silk covered the walls. A servant deposited *liqueurs* and cake upon a small table, and left them alone.

They were neither of them inclined to sleep. La Valliere, especially, was too excited even to think. De Brie was startled by what had passed between his friend and the Count. He seated himself before the fire, the bright-leaping flames of which seemed spirits and denizens of an ethereal life.

'You were not jesting with the Count?'
he said.

'Jesting!' said la Valliere. 'I saw him
—the Abbé—as I see you.'

'I believe you. The wonder is, not
that you saw him, but that we, all of us, see
so little. The whole of Nature is ensouled.
There is no such thing as matter, as material
existence. Everything is instinct with the
nature of God, or of the Enemy of God.'

La Valliere did not reply. He sat looking listlessly into the fire, seeing perhaps
in the dancing flames the face of the
Countess Eve.

'We have entered into a new life,'
de Brie went on. 'The old centuries
slumbered in a shadowy dream-life, a life
of the unseen and of the soul. They had

the truth, but they did not know it; we know it, but have lost its possession. I have often thought, but to-night it comes upon me with an irresistible certainty, that you are in yourself at once the embodiment of both—of the mystical life of the past centuries, and of the material life of to-day. You have the ignorant instinct of the past towards the unseen and the ideal; and you have the animal instinct of the present, untrammelled by the new-born conscience and responsibility which, in most men, stands in the way of the moral *abandon* which is necessary for the magnetic union with the unseen. To you, if to no one else, it should assume palpable form.'

'You do not seem very complimentary,'

said la Valliere dreamily. 'Have you more to say?'

It was not the first time that he had listened to such lengthy dissertations from his friend.

'You always remind me,' de Brie went on, 'of those old Greek natures, half human, half fay, to whom belonged the secrets of Nature and of the sky, of the elements and of the spirit-world—pure animals such as we see among us now, our dogs and falcons, the creatures of their training and circumstances, but how perfect of their kind!'

'Really,' said la Valliere, laughing and rousing himself from his indolent attitude before the blazing fire, 'you are more and more polite. Dogs and falcons! What next, I wonder?'

De Brie sat looking at him with that unique and inexplicable attraction which exists only between man and man, and very often between men of singularly opposite nature and opinion ; but indeed la Valliere's attraction was so great that it was almost impossible to see him without admiration. He stood with his back to the stately hearth, the festooned walls of the room, the flowered-silk hangings and tapestries aglow with the fitful light. The finely-cut, delicate features, the lofty grace of pose and manner, were never more apparent to his friend than on this night. His heart yearned more than ever towards the matchless fascination of this facile, attractive nature — plastic as clay in the potter's hand, and yet attractive as though it had absorbed the grace of all natures into its own.

'He is nothing in himself,' he thought; 'he is nothing but a lovely masque. This highly - strung, sympathetic nature, this magnetic temperament, this careless, happy, Greek conscience and unshackled will and purpose, confined by no scruple, bounded by no law — to what fell use might it not be put? How perfect and beautiful an instrument and dwelling-place for a malefic spirit to use and to inhabit!'

. . . . .

And this stately house that seemed to him so empty, so swept and garnished for the delight of such few persons as he had seen to inhabit it, what was it but the stage of a concourse of beings, the scene of a conflict terrible and enduring as life and the grave? Alone! we are never alone. Dead! nothing dies. The dead ancestor lives again in the so-called innocent child. The foul deed, the craven act, the sensual sin, stands out suddenly face to face with the pale, saintly girl, and confuses and mars her life. 'Alone! we are never alone!'

He said these words aloud, for there came into his mind a sudden sense of supreme mystery, even of terror—of the infinite consequence of the next moment's action and word. A sense of dominant and all but overpowering, malefic force, of the need of prayer and of rescue. Vaguely as in a dream, dimly as in the distant past, he seemed conscious of the birth of sin—

conscious of committed sin which, through the long process of time, was at that moment, by some fatal necromancy, drawing himself and la Valliere and the Countess Eve, and all whom he knew, within its netted toils.   He too rose from his seat.

La Valliere was standing on the hearth, his figure thrown into strong relief by the firelight, by the contrasted shine and gloom.   His face, usually so suave and placid, had a scared and set look.

' De Brie,' he said, ' do you remember that night at Mesmer's in Paris, when the girl who is so like the Queen was in a trance, and you dragged me away, and you said that it was not a girl but a fiend? Something like that is in this house—now.'

'I took you away from Mesmer's,' said de Brie, 'because I knew that it could not be the Queen, though it was so like her. I said it was a devilish delusion and the work of a fiend.'

'They are here,' said la Valliere, now with some bitterness in his tone. 'You are a saint; they will not suffer you to see or to feel them near. They know that it is useless to tempt you — but they are here.'

'If any of us are tempted, if the house be haunted by evil spirits,' said de Brie, 'let us kneel down and pray.' And without waiting to see whether la Valliere followed his example or not, he knelt down and recited a prayer, not long before used at the jubilee of 1751.

'O Father of light and God of all truth, purge the whole world from all errors, abuses, corruptions, and sins. Beat down the standard of Satan, and set up everywhere the standard of Christ. Abolish the reign of sin, and establish the kingdom of grace in all hearts. Let humility triumph over pride and ambition; charity over hatred, envy, and malice; purity and temperance over lust and excess; meekness over passion, and disinterestedness and poverty of spirit over covetousness and the love of this perishable world. Let the gospel of Christ, in faith and practice, prevail throughout the world.'

De Brie rose from his knees and looked at his friend. Whether la Valliere had knelt or not he did not know, but the scared look was gone out of his eyes.

'It is time we went to bed,' he said. 'To-morrow we must get back into the city, somehow. I have a rehearsal at eleven o'clock.'

.   .   .   .   .

In his unsettled sleep that night de Brie had a dream.

He dreamt that he was in a valley, in the moonlight, in an autumn night. On the grassy slopes and in the rocky paths of the valley, in the mystic light, number-less shadowy figures were walking, stray-ing up and down, carrying branches of palms, olives and willows. The cold, cruel light of the moon — dead, pitiless and chill, in foil and enmity to the warm

E

and life-giving sunlight, cast black and deathlike shadows from the trees and moving, flitting forms.

It seemed to de Brie that he stood for some time regarding these people with wonder. Then he was conscious that one with a mocking vizard that concealed his face stood by his side, and he asked him, 'Who are these? and what do they do?'

And the fantastic mime answered—

'These are Hebrews. They seek, on the seventh day of the Feast of Tabernacles, for the "shadow of the shadow," for so their Rabbis teach them out of Deuteronomy. "Their shadow is departed from them." This does not relate, they tell them, to the natural shadow,

which any one can see, but to the "shadow
of the shadow," the reflection of the first,
which is given only to the elect.'

'And do these see it?' asked de Brie.

'No,' said the masque, with a rippling,
mocking laughter in his tone. 'Watch
and see.'

And it seemed to de Brie that, as he
still looked, the fantastic figures were not
only those of Hebrews, but appeared in
the dress and shapes of all peoples and
races, and that among them were many
whom de Brie knew; and in the white
moonlight, that drew such terrible sharp
black shadows, the distant drives and
vistas of the wood, which was in itself
weird and cabalistical, and haunted by
such strange forms, became peopled by

a throng of shapes and figures more spectral and shadowy still, and resounded with echoing footsteps more uncertain and remote, all deriving their existence from these shadows, and from these wandering, pacing forms, who, still carrying their branches of palms and olives and willows, continued their fantastic search ; and the sins of the fathers were reproduced in the children, and phantoms, that were at once shadowy and evil, gave birth to phantoms more shadowy and evil still.

And de Brie said to the masquer at his side—

'This is a great mystery, that matter can beget spirit, a fleshly lust beget intellect, sin beget a being capable of, but missing, a divine life.'

And the mocking demon by his side laughed, and said—

' By a kind of necromancy a man's shadow has been known to walk and talk of itself ; but *its* shadow ! what is that ? '

And the strange moonlit dance went on solemnly, as with a set purpose, but futile in result and in fruit, and de Brie said—

' Is there then no hope for these ? '

And the mime by his side took off his masque, and de Brie woke at the horror of his face, and in his waking ear were the scornful words—

' There is none.'

And with a start he awoke to the fresh spring morning and the light.

WHEN the young men awoke they found
that their windows looked out upon a
prospect of soft and tranquil loveliness,
quiet and peaceful as a happy dream.
Immediately below the windows was a
terrace, and beyond the terrace an orchard
of fruit trees, then leafless, but just breaking into blossom, the twisted branches gray
with lichens and sparkling with dewdrops ;
and beyond this again a stretch of park·
and pastures and vineyards, and then, in the
far distance, the Jura Mountains, with their
dark fir forests and escarpments of white

rocks. Between the windows and these distant hills shadowy gradations of light revealed the ridges of vineyard and woodland with a delicate, faint tracery of outline, and a clear distinctness, in the softly-tinted morning air. It seemed to de Brie's troubled waking-sense that such a dawn as this might have broke over that other Paradise in the first mornings of the world.

An early meal was served to the young men, and a carriage conveyed them to the city, where, as la Valliere had said, they had to attend the rehearsal of a new play.

To the intelligent actor there is something strangely suggestive and fascinating in this correlation of parts, when the affairs of that which most men consent to call

real life are placed in close connection, are
contrasted with, perhaps incorporated into,
the ideal world of creative art.

This interwoven tissue of fancy and
action made la Valliere's world, already
fantastic and bizarre, more fantastic still.
The characters upon the stage mingled
with his conception of those he met with
in the streets and houses of the city.
Nothing seemed strange or impossible to
him, nothing surprised him.   The peculiar
charm of his acting consisted in the fact that .
it was not acting—the stage was as real to
him as life, life as real to him as the stage.

The play in which he was now taking a
part was one of those intensely French
pieces which no audience except a French
one, if it were not the audience which

applauded Terence, could possibly have appreciated. The strain upon an actor in such a piece, the interest of which consists entirely in dialogue and chiefly in repartee and *équivoque*—repartee, it is true, exquisitely appropriate to the individual character, but still simply repartee—is tremendous, especially before an audience which recognises and appreciates the faintest *nuance* of character and phrase.

La Valliere came out of the theatre exhausted, even shattered both in mind and body. The excitement of the past night, the Countess with her sudden and unexpected look, the strange figure by the couch with its terribly irresistible influence, the restless sleep troubled with dreams, the glimpse of Paradise in the early dawn, all

this had strung his mind and wrought his
body to a pitch of nervous excitement.
The singular correlative condition of existence as it appeared to him, the constantly
reiterated point and antithesis of the
dialogue in which he had taken part, and
the strange antithesis and uncertainty of
the real and the fictional—which might
be the one and which the other—dogging
his footsteps in the life of every day, produced a condition which was not far short
of delirium.   When he left the playhouse
he wandered restlessly about the streets.

Not far from the theatre, stretching
westward from the gate by which the
friends had left the city the night before
and returned to it in the morning, the glacis
of the old walls had been planted with rows

of trees, now of considerable size. Along
one of these shaded paths, at that time of
the day almost deserted, la Valliere took
his way.

The peaceful scene that stretched before his eyes, the vista of bare, intricately-
woven branches, the grass-bordered paths,
the quiet figures dotted here and there,
soothed his wearied senses and lured his
imagination to retrace once more the startling fantasies of the past night. Once more
he sat by the bright wood fire in the château;
once more the strange birds and flowers of
the fantastic screen quivered before his
eyes ; once more he saw that slight, perfect
form, that lovely face, lean eagerly forward
as if to meet him—a sight that no man who
had once seen it could easily forget; once

more, but now fainter and more uncertain, he saw the intruding figure of the Abbé, if it were an abbé, and his heart beat suddenly with an intense longing that this entrancing scene might again take form in substance and in fact.

As this longing became more intense, and he slowly paced the straight, tree-bordered path, it flashed suddenly upon his recollection that it was *only* when the strange visitant had stolen softly from out of the darkness, and had spoken, or had appeared to speak, to the unconscious Countess, that she had manifested any interest whatever in himself. However she might have been attracted by la Valliere's acting, and have wished to make his acquaintance, yet, as the evening drew on, her manner, so far as it had shown any interest at all, had seemed to concentrate itself entirely on de Brie. It was not till after this mysterious intercourse that her manner had changed, and her heart had seemed to entertain new aspirations and new desires.

As this thought occurred to la Valliere with greater and still greater certainty of recollection, it seemed that his longing changed, and that an intense desire formed itself in his mind to see this strange personage again, as though he felt that it was through its mediation, and this only, that his object could be obtained. But along all the distant vista of straight walk and grassy verge, no such figure, intensely as he sought it, met his gaze.

But it seemed singular, even to la Valliere's excited thought, that, though this strange medium was absent, the scene by the fireside repeated itself with a surprising freshness and intensity in his fancy, an intensity so overpowering as to absorb all his faculties in a burning desire to see it again enacted; and, by a curious reaction, into a settled purpose to see—almost a prayer that he might see—this mysterious figure once more. 'Whoever, whatever it might be, from above or from below, be it good or evil,' the concentrated will seemed to cry, 'Appear! show yourself again!'

But down the long alleys, and through the thickly-planted trees, there was still no sign.

He had by this time reached a bend of the fortified fosse which concealed the city more completely from sight, and as far as his eye could reach, the glacis was even more absolutely solitary than before. In the distance, where the wall turned again, the quaint, sharp turrets of a city gate cut the misty pallor of the sky. Between la Valliere and this distant object, over the long stretch of glacis and planted walk, not a single figure could be seen.

He advanced some way along the silent avenue, and an overpowering feeling impressed his senses that something was near. It seemed that through the veil of sunny ether that surrounded him some strange personality was approaching, and endeavouring to make itself visible ; an excited desperation of feeling, of mingled apprehension and desire, of attraction and repulsion, resolved itself finally into a fixed determination to *see*.

The next moment, by the third tree from him on the right hand, la Valliere saw the Abbé again.

He seemed to advance towards la Valliere with an insinuating gesture and attitude, and that singular sensation, as of the presence of a masque, forced itself again upon his mind, a masqued form, a masqued nature, a masqued purpose; and in a singularly curious way there seemed, on the part of the stranger, to exist a feeling which corresponded with the feeling in la Valliere's mind; on his part a suave, attractive friendliness, and yet a craven fear; on la Valliere's part, a desire at one moment to meet the singular visitant half-way, at the next an equally strong impulse to turn and flee from him—a complicated dual impression which, one would surely think, must involve the two in a hopeless mesh and net of intricate wandering and loss.

As la Valliere awaited his approach the Abbé seemed about to speak more than once, or possibly he did speak without la Valliere's being able to catch a sound; but at last something like the faintest soft whisper, a courteous and persuasive voice, was perceptible to his sense, and he seemed to hear these words—

'If Monsieur Felix la Valliere will go to the vesper service at the Convent of

Our Lady of Pity this evening, at five o'clock, he will find his friend Monsieur de Brie, and he will also see another friend.'

'And the other friend?' la Valliere himself seemed to say in the same hushed undertone.

'Is Madame la Comtesse du Pic-Adam?'

'If I am not mistaken,' said la Valliere, still concentrating all his power of will to keep the figure of the Abbé within his sense of vision and to hear his voice— 'if I am not mistaken I have had the pleasure already of seeing Monsieur l'Abbé at the château of Monsieur le Comte, but, what was somewhat singular, Monsieur le Comte assured me that he was unconscious of his presence.'

A most striking and singular expres-

sion formed itself upon the other's face—
an expression compounded of mocking
amusement, or what would have been
amusement in other men, and an unspeak-
ably malefic and vindictive look.

'I am nevertheless well acquainted
with Monsieur le Comte, and he with me,'
said the fair-spoken yet malefic voice. 'I
may even in some sense claim him as my
parent or perhaps my *parrain.*'

To la Valliere's excited fancy, trained
as it was to detect play and parody upon
words, a singular ambiguity seemed to
lurk in this speech, more so than perhaps
the words might warrant.

'*Parrain,*' he said, 'may mean, I believe, either a godfather or a soldier
appointed to be the executioner of his

comrade.   I trust that this is not the function of Monsieur l'Abbé.'

'It may come even to that,' the baleful voice replied.

There was a pause.   In spite of la Valliere's intense desire to see and hear, the figure became every moment more indistinct—the voice fainter.

'Monsieur la Valliere will not fail to attend the vespers this evening,' — the empty, misty air seemed full of the soft yet mocking words,—'and above all things let him remember to be bold.'

The empty air must have produced the sound, for down the long perspective of terraced walk, as far as the distant pinnacles of the city gate, no form or figure could be seen.

LA VALLIERE did not fail to attend the
vesper service at the Convent of Our
Lady of Pity the same afternoon. The
nuns used the parish church, to which
their convent adjoined, for their service,
and as their singing was extremely good,
the vesper service was the fashionable
lounge of the city idlers of both sexes.

When la Valliere entered the church
a considerable portion of the nave was
occupied by a numerous audience, seated
upon chairs. Pausing for a few moments
on the outskirts of this crowd he at last

perceived a group, near the antique screen
that stretched in front of the chancel,
that seemed familiar to him. Making his
way quietly round the edge of the crowd,
he found that this group consisted of the
Countess, accompanied by two girls, of
his friend de Brie, of two young officers
of the regiment in garrison whom he had
already met, and of a little old Vicomte, a
cadet of a noble family in the neighbourhood, a man notorious for existing simply
for the purpose of retailing to one acquaintance after another the last scandal-
ous story he could hear or invent.

'Ah, Monsieur la Valliere,' he whispered, as soon as the young actor approached him, after addressing the others,
'how pale the lovely Countess looks!

Fancy that old don of a husband of hers, instead of hastening with her to Paris, settling down in this villainous little town, which I have described in a word as stupidity personified. Not bad, was it? No wonder she looks *ennuyée*. How could she be otherwise with that monster of a husband, cold as his own snow-peak? He is doubtless right. She would not be his long in Paris. Besides he is a great man here. She looks to you, *mon ami*, to *se désennuyer.'*

He did not think it necessary to tell la Valliere that he had given precisely the same advice to both the young officers, and used the same words exactly, at a *déjeuner* in the city at which he had been present that morning.

The parish church in which the nuns sang was an ancient Gothic structure of the thirteenth century, at the time we are speaking of very much neglected and decayed. The pavement of the nave was broken and uneven, and the hand of time had softened every carved column and sculptured tomb to a gracious mellowness of outline. The short spring day was drawing to a close, and behind the lofty rood-screen, with its towering crucifix, dark shadows, thrown from the lights of distant altars, brooded over the space beyond, and ascended to the lofty, foliated roofs and to the arcades of the aisles. The gigantic, reedlike pillars of the nave loomed vaguely in the sombre light.

The Countess had chosen a seat near one of these massive pillars, by which she sat together with the two girls, her companions. The old Vicomte and the two officers, who were both noble, sat immediately behind them, and de Brie and la Valliere still farther back; but the arrangement of the chairs around the column left a clear space between the two young men and the Countess, which it was easy to overpass.

From the grated gallery of the nuns, beyond the shadowy veil of screen and crucifix, floated down the soft, melodious harmonies of women's voices, in wave after wave of delicate sound, like the measured refrain of an angelic choir—

'Missus est Gabriel angelus.'

The notes fell upon de Brie's mind with a sense of peace and calm, pure and undefiled by stain of earth as was the heart of that Holy Maiden to whom the Angel Gabriel was sent.

It would be difficult to find greater divergence of motive than that which had brought the two friends to the same place and service. De Brie constantly attended the vespers of the nuns. He had even composed music which they had sung. He came partly from love of the music, partly because the sacredness of the place and of the words was congenial to his spirit, which found and heard in every incident and sound of daily life something holy and inspiring, something that left the spirit better and more refined than before.

Himself a skilled musician, he had never for a moment lost the divine message of music in the outward form. Music was to him not a scientifically balanced system of notes. It was an infinite and eternal voice speaking to the soul of man.

We know something of the motives which have brought la Valliere to the service. He had been present before, in accordance with the fashion of the city in which, for a time, he found himself. To-day, however, he came from no motives of fashion; his mind and senses were lost in a chaos of excitement, and of conflicting strifes and ideas.

The *Stabat Mater* was being sung to a motet which de Brie himself had written for the nuns. In the contrast between its sad strains and the fashionable assemblage there was something which, at the moment, struck his fancy with a sense of reality ; even the rustling of silk, the slight noises, the occasional whisper, did not jar upon his ear, rather they seemed to him part of the great mystery of sound, and of the mystery which sound conveys.

> ' Sancta Mater, istud agas,
> Crucifixi fige plagas
> Cordi meo valide.
> Tui Nati vulnerati
> Tam dignati pro me pati
> Pœnas mecum divide.'

The mystery that transmutes, with a wondrous alchemy, the long, weary hours of pain into the happiest life ; the mystery of sacrifice and of pain ; the mystery which is in itself a personal, plastic Force ; the mystery expressed in sound by concerted discord,—must surely be able to absorb into itself the frivolous and disturbing elements of life.

He was engaged, rapt in an ecstasy of wonder and delight, in forming more ex- quisitely-suggestive chords, if any such existed, by which these ideas might, if possible, be adequately expressed, when he was suddenly startled by la Valliere's hand laid upon his arm.

'Do you know that abbé who is stand- ing by the pillar speaking to Madame la Comtesse?'

'Abbé?' replied de Brie crossly, 'you are dreaming; there is no one there. There is no one by the pillar speaking to the Countess.'

'No one!' said la Valliere beneath

his breath. 'No one! Do you mean to tell me that you do not see him? and she is listening to him too! Look! she turns her head!'

It was true. The Countess at that moment, inspired apparently by some sudden impulse, turned in her seat and fixed her eyes with an expression of kindly appeal full on la Valliere's face.

The *Stabat Mater* had ceased, and there was a moment's hush of delicious sound. La Valliere rose from his seat, and as he rose he was conscious, wild and unsettled as his thoughts were, that the figure of the Abbé faded suddenly from his sight and disappeared behind the massive, carved pillar. Scarcely knowing what he did, *la Valliere took his place.*

'You have seen too little of Paradise,
Monsieur la Valliere,' the Countess was
saying in her softest voice and most
courteous manner.   'You   must   return
soon, even at this time of year.'

'Entrance into Paradise is hardly for
us mortals, Madame la Comtesse,' replied
la Valliere in a soft voice.   'The beauty
dazzles us, the fine air is too pure for us
to breathe ; we faint and die in the unac-
customed life.'

'You are too modest,' said the Countess
with a gracious, winning smile.   'We will
not treat you so badly as that.   What
pledge of welcome shall I give you ?'

'There is only one key to Paradise,
Madame,' said la Valliere, still in a soft
undertone.   'Only one spell by which the

gates fall open, and the happy visitant walks the sunny paths void of fear and at ease. That key is love.'

As he spoke these words the nuns began the antiphon before the Magnificat, *Magnum Hæreditatis Mysterium*, and the congregation became silent once more. The Countess looked full in la Vallière's face as she sat back in her chair.

Surely a great 'mystery of inheritance' that Paradise should open with the key of love! For a moment a look of eager inquiry and hope came into her eyes, then a sudden, dark shade passed over her lovely face, which relapsed into the look of wearied sadness that was habitual to it.

'You are right,' she said softly; 'there is no Paradise without love.'

'Missus est Gabriel angelus,' the nuns had sung. Pure and holy as was the story of that heaven-born messenger, it was not more pure than the thoughts that passed through her own heart as she listened to the alluring, monotonous strain. The weight of a grievous disappointment was pressing her down, the weight of her husband's melancholy and icy reserve, more frozen, as it seemed, from the occasional futile effort to cast it off cr to conceal it, —a weight the more insupportable because its real origin and cause was unknown to her — one of those 'mysteries of inheritance' which defile the ground-springs of life, and which waste and mar our loves.

'There is no key to Paradise save that of love'; they were strange and searching

words—that its paths were only peaceful
and happy with love — that without love
the heart died of famine in the empty air.
How true they were! How well she
knew them to be true!

They were spoken by an elegant and
polished stranger, a trained. actor on the
stage of life, every tone and word and
gesture nicely chosen for the attaining of
his end, possessed of every art and trick
of tone and manner to please the heart and
ear. 'The only key to Paradise was
love.' What had she done to forfeit her
husband's love? What should she do
now that Paradise might be hers, really
hers ; not as walking its paths as a chance
stranger only, but as the owner and mistress of the enchanting scene? What part

was this pleasant friend destined to play in her life?— he that had so suddenly appeared in her paths accompanied with such strange suggestive thoughts and emotions within herself? He had seemed to help her already. Should she trust to his friendliness for further aid?

But there was another whose thoughts were troubled among the thoughtless audience and amidst the wealth of lovely sound. De Brie had been startled out of his musical reverie of pious musing by la Valliere's strange assertion, and by the coincidence which followed and seemed to substantiate it — the singular fact that the Countess should at that moment turn her inviting gaze upon his friend. A sense of mystery, of the presence of felt but unseen influences, oppressed him with a feeling of apprehension, almost of dread. Something terrible — so it seemed to him — might happen at any time. Around the outskirts of the human crowd, Powers inimical to human virtue, perhaps even to human life, seemed to hover, invisible and impalpable, ready at any moment to concentrate their inherent powers, the power of beings purely intellectual, for the working of their own malefic ends. What could he do to stem this evil? to defeat this plot against human happiness? to deliver those who were bound, whom Satan would lead captive at his will?

> 'Holy Mother of Redemption,
> By that Ave Gabriel brought,
> By the blessing of that Ave
> Sinners kneel to Thee!'

The concluding antiphon of the season was being sung by the nuns.

The congregation streamed out on to the *pavé* of the churchyard, surrounded by the lofty, gabled houses of the old city, to a strange light—the solemn, evening sky of spring, the flambeaux of the servants, and the glimmer from the houses shining on the wet flags. The old Viscount conducted the Countess to her carriage, to which the girls who were her companions followed her. As she entered she turned to la Valliere, who was close by, and said some words to him in a low voice. As the carriage drove off la Valliere turned back into the churchyard to rejoin his friend. De Brie was late in leaving the church, having remained in prayer, and la Valliere met him at the west door.

Then, in the fitful, uncertain, flickering light, as he turned to accompany his friend, close to the spot the Countess's coach had just left, by the side of the paved pathway to the gate, and beneath a quaint iron standard containing an oil-lamp, he saw the Abbé again, his face fully turned towards the young men.

'Claude!' he cried, passionately seizing his friend by the arm; 'there he is again —the Abbé whom you will not see. You shall see him. There, by the lamp!'

He held de Brie by the arm, and unconsciously exerted all the force of his vivid and intense personality upon the consciousness of his dearest friend, with

whom he had been brought up from child-
hood, the sympathy with whose spirit was
closer than that with any of his own
kindred.   'Claude, you shall see him.
There, by the lamp!'

De Brie's attitude seemed to stiffen, as
though a motive-power not his own ran
through his frame.   He turned his eyes in
the direction pointed out to him, and in
a moment the pupils dilated into a fixed
and terror-stricken gaze.   A look of horror
and of intense distrust and repulsion dead-
ened the colour of his face into a ghastly
white.   He gasped for breath, and clutch-
ing wildly at la Valliere's arm, he sank
senseless on to the paved footway.

THE two girls thought that the Countess was very quiet as she drove home. When they found that their chatter was unheeded they subsided into silence, and the Countess sat looking steadfastly before her, the words of la Valliere still ringing in her ears. 'There is no entrance into Paradise without love.' These words mingled with tones of the nun's singing, with the clear altos and trebles which recited the sorrows of the Mother of God. Was all that long-past story nothing but a metaphor of the hours that were present to her, and to all?

There were pure virgins now to whom the angel of God came; could there possibly be a second Eve?

She left the two girls at their home without the city gate, and on her arrival at the château, went up at once into the private suite of apartments, where she expected to find her husband. Young as she was she heard a voice speaking to her, that told her that a crisis in her life was near; that it behoved her to be careful of her steps; that, above all things, as she might hope to respect herself hereafter, it was incumbent upon her to see her husband at once, that very night. What might happen, she, poor child, could not tell. Any way, she would be there—would speak to him, would show herself by his side.

The apartments which the Count and Countess occupied consisted of four or five rooms, terminating in a cabinet, formed in a small projecting angle of the front, and containing a staircase leading into the private garden.

As the Countess passed through the intervening rooms a vague sense of depression weighed upon her mind. On every side of her, as she passed, nothing met her eyes but such objects as were calculated to soothe and to please. The walls were wreathed with carving of fruit and flowers in strong relief, framing in the midst of their own loveliness portraits and landscapes more lovely than themselves; and below were buffets and presses full of strange and beautiful and curious things.

The old major-domo accompanied the Countess.

'Monsieur le Comte,' he said, 'was in the little cabinet at the end of the suite.' He believed that he was there, because he himself had been into the privy garden, to speak to one of the gardeners, and Monsieur was not there.

At these words, as it seemed, a still deeper apprehension and dread, more insupportable because so inexplicable, troubled the Countess's mind.

'Have you seen Monsieur since the morning?' she said.

'I attended Monsieur le Comte *après le déjeuner*," said the old servant. 'He appeared to me distrait and absorbed.'

Drawing a heavy curtain that screened

a door opening into the cabinet, the major-
domo bowed, and left his mistress to pro-
ceed alone.

She stood for a moment with clasped
hands before her, herself the most perfect
object in a world of beauty on every
side.

As she stood, in her bright, fanciful
dress, somewhat disordered by her afternoon drive, with a delicate beauty and a
refinement of outline and of feature that
made her, as she stood, so perfect a picture in her beautiful house, there rose once
again in her heart, amid the *entourage* of
luxury and splendour and fine living, a
genuine longing and desire, common to the
loftiest and the humblest life—the same in
the cottage as in the palace—a longing for

love, a desire towards that which is, of all things, most to be desired, a life of pure and holy domestic love. ' Missus est Gabriel angelus ' the nuns had sung. The sweet tones, the mystic words, haunted her sense, and seemed to teach her something beyond her sense, beyond all thought and hope of hers, beyond all the thought and hope of men.

The door of the cabinet was open, and she stopped for a moment before going in. The Count was seated, with his back to her, at a table at which apparently he had been writing. The room was lighted with candles, but the curtains of the windows were still undrawn, and outside a brilliant moon revealed the garden and the distant wooded fields in a faint vision of delicate

forms and lines; but what the Countess
saw, in a sudden vision that absorbed all
her faculties, was neither the Count, nor
the room, nor the faint moonlit distance,
etched as it were upon the dark background of night, but what her intense
mental sympathy, her pure love for her
husband, revealed to her as that which at
the same moment was present to his own
mental gaze.

His form was fixed and rigid, and his
gaze appeared concentrated upon the land-
scape without.

'I never see her, never see her.' It
was the Count speaking, though the voice
was scarcely his own, so strange and faint
it seemed. 'Never see her, and yet she
must be always near me.'

It was evident that, no more than the Countess, did he see the objects that were really before his eyes.

She saw, as she stopped sudden and still upon the threshold of the room, plain and distinct in vision before her eyes, a dark lake, wild and vast and dreary, lying as it were in eternal gloom ; the chill, terrible waters, motionless with the stillness of a settled despair, black with unfathomable mysteries of the dim æons of existence when the world lay void and misty and slimy in the pangs of creation ; and over the lake, indistinct in mystic shadow, pinewood and forest dingle, and, still higher, the rocky scars and shoulders of the great hills, and then a belt of mist and cloudland, and then, high against the azure sky,

serene, impassive, not of this earth, amid
the solemn unapproachable dawns and the
celestial sunsets, cold and terrible as a
dream, pure and lovely as a saint, pallid,
lofty, wonderful, the stainless form of a
peak of snow.

'I never see her,' said the Count
again; 'never see her, yet she must be
near.'

The Countess sank on her knees beside
her husband's chair, her hands resting upon
the carved arms.   Between her and him
there seemed to rise an impassable barrier
—nay, rather a positive, active presence, a
dividing force.   He seemed unconscious
even that she was there.   He did not
move, nothing moved, nothing happened.
It seemed, indeed, impossible that any-

thing could ever happen any more—hence the terrible, the hopeless despair.

The Countess rose slowly from the ground, stood for a second upon the threshold—then she left the room.

DE BRIE was carried back into the church, and from thence, as he did not recover consciousness, into the visitors' room of the convent ; but it was a long time before he came to himself. When he had recollected himself a shudder of horror passed over his frame, and he absolutely refused to tell what he had seen.

' Do not ask me what I saw,' he said.

' He has received,' said the doctor, sententiously, 'a tremendous moral shock, which has for a moment annihilated his rational sense. It is in such cases as these that we may hope to gain an insight, the only one it would seem that we can gain, into the relationship of the seen with the unseen. By witnessing such startling events we seem to be placed *en rapport* with powers and influences outside our everyday life.'

De Brie seemed so shattered and ill that he was removed into an adjoining room, where the doctor directed that he should be left in perfect quiet, visited at intervals only by one of ·the nursing sisters. As he became more composed he requested to be allowed to see the Abbess, saying that he had something of the utmost importance to communicate to her.

The Abbess came into the room, and they were left alone. She was a beautiful woman of early middle life, tall, and of dignified appearance. She had suffered, and knew how to pity the suffering. It was not the first time that she had seen de Brie. He had even, as we have seen, composed music which had been sung by the nuns.

'You have something of great import-ance to communicate to me, my son,' she said.

'My mother,' said de Brie, 'do not ask me what I saw. I cannot tell you what I saw. It seemed to me that I saw a vision, a foul and terrible vision—as far as words can faintly image what I saw—ghastly with the horrors of the charnel-house and the grave, with all the foulness of cor-ruption and with all the horror of de-spair, a figure, gaunt with the terrors of a skeleton, and the grewsome pallor of a shroud. It seemed to me that I saw for a moment's span all that evil could work of ravin, that innocence could suffer of defilement, that fair fame and prospects could endure of disappointment and delusion. I cannot tell you what I saw.'

The Abbess was seated at some distance from de Brie, who had risen from his couch and was seated upon the edge of it, his hands clasped before him, very pale, and troubled in mind, hardly able to control his voice.

' My mother,' he went on after a pause, 'some terrible evil is menacing my dearest friend, la Valliere, and it connects itself with the Comtesse du Pic-Adam. Some fatal misfortune will befall both of them

unless aid can be found. She appears to
be estranged from her husband, to whom
she has been so recently married, by some
mysterious fate or reason, some strange
dividing power that stands between them.
She is attracted towards la Valliere by as
mysterious a force. La Valliere is good,
amiable, true, but he is the slave of his
feelings, carried away by the passion of
the moment; a born actor, to whom all
parts are alike. They are lost unless some
help may be found. Were it possible to
discover the reason of the Count's strange
absorption much would be gained.'

Some deep emotion disturbed the
Abbess's mind. She became absolutely
pale, and seemed, after a moment's conflict
of hesitation, to arrive at a resolve which

involved self-sacrifice and some unspeakable effort and pain. A slight shudder
passed over her figure as she spoke.

'My son,' she said, 'I know and confide in you. I know that you are pure
in heart and life, a good Catholic, a true
son of the Church. I will confide all to
you. I can reveal the mystery that over-
shadows the Comte and Comtesse du Pic-
Adam, and which has drawn your friend
into its fatal meshes. It is a sad story of
woman's frailty. It will rend my heart to
tell it. It is my duty to tell it to you,
and to suffer in the telling. It is a penance, which is but part of a life of penance,
much of which, I begin to fear, has been
self-appointed and mischosen, and therefore ineffectual and even pernicious. This

penance is of God's appointment.   It shall
be borne.   May God in His mercy accept
it, and make it efficient and fruitful to the
salvation of His creatures from the snare
of the Fiend.   You tell me that the
Countess is estranged from her husband;
I will tell you why.'

De Brie gazed at the Abbess with
astonishment. His mind, already unsettled
and disturbed, was still further perplexed
by this strange and unexpected announce-
ment.   He almost doubted his own sanity
and that of the Abbess.   He seemed to be
wandering in a wild, unhallowed dream.

'Twenty years ago,' began the Abbess,
'there was a young girl.   She lived with a
great and noble lady, her patroness and mistress—Madame la Comtesse du Pic-Adam.'

The Abbess lingered over this name as though she loved it, and yet at the same time spoke it with effort and reluctance. She paused for a moment to gather strength and resolve before she went on.

'From the top of the Jura heights, which you can see from the château of the Count, you may discern, on a very clear day, beyond the nearer snowpeaks of the Alps, a distant peak clear and sharp against the sky. Beneath this peak this young girl lived, in the château of her mistress, in one of the valley-passes dropping down into Italy. The Comtes du Pic-Adam were French. Some ances-tor, a soldier in the French armies of invasion, had married the daughter of a small noble and settled down on his estate,

calling himself, as his father-in-law had
done, by the name of the snowpeak that
rose above his valley, and of which strange
tales of a supernatural spirit-world were
told by the peasants. They believed that
our father Adam, wandering from Paradise,
with all the world before him in which to
choose a place of rest, had climbed this
inaccessible peak, and had held supreme
council, if not with God Himself, at least
with celestial messengers and spirits, as to
his future course. The descendants of this
French soldier, in later and more peace-
able times, called themselves French, and
served the French king, both at home and
abroad.

'Of all the great and noble ladies
whom God has sent into this world to

beautify His creation, to glorify His name, and for the relief and happiness of His suffering creatures, none ever fulfilled the object of their Creator more fully than did Madame la Comtesse du Pic-Adam. If any man had, by the snare of Satan, come to doubt the existence of a merciful God, or had suffered himself to believe or to conclude that righteousness and virtue were empty names, that unselfishness and sacrifice were a foolish dream, and that human nature differs nothing from the nature of the beasts that perish, he had only to know Madame la Comtesse for one day, for one hour even, and he changed his mind. The mountain peaks were not more pure and stainless than was her mind, nor so lofty nor so near to heaven

as were her thoughts; and the chiefest
ministering angel could scarcely be more
touched by the sorrows of humanity, more
ready or more constant in help.   As she
moved about her household, or among the
cottages of the poor, or upon the terraces
of her hill-gardens, or in the great halls or
amid the brilliant crowds of castles and
cities, she did not seem like a being of
this world.   This young girl worshipped
her as a saint of God.'

The Abbess paused, as though the task
she had set herself was wellnigh beyond
her power.   Then she went on.   De Brie
held his breath in nervous strain.

'This lady had an only son, the Comte
du Pic-Adam whom you know.   He had
been educated at home, under tutors, but

he was afterwards sent with his *gouverneur* to Paris and other cities. His mother was ambitious, as far as he was concerned. She was descended from a family of higher nobility than her husband was, and she wished her son to take a higher place in the court and in the world than his family had ever filled, and above all things that he should marry within *la haute noblesse.* All this the young girl knew.

'The young Count came home. As might be expected, he was very much changed by his foreign life. He seemed, however, to be thoroughly true and affectionate to his mother, and of gallant and lofty aspirations and desires. He was very handsome and perfectly bred.

'Madame la Comtesse du Pic-Adam

was of that noblest of natures which never suspects evil. More than in any one else she believed and trusted in the young girl, whom she had brought up, whom she had all but created, upon whom she had lavished the wealth of her love and the dower of her great example, all that was in her power to bestow of enjoyment and of instruction in all the arts that make life happy, the hours golden, the possessor fortunate. The young Count saw in this young girl something that pleased his fancy. He spoke to her kindly of his journeyings. He met her at every turn. He used to hunt in the forests and on the craggy rocks where the chamois haunt; but he used to come back earlier than was supposed, and the young girl knew where to

meet him, by chance, in the lower terraces
of the gardens, by the woods.   I have no
power to go on, but there is no need.'

There was a short deathlike pause.
Then the Abbess spoke again.

'One terrible, one fatal night, the
Countess had been on a visit to a neighbouring town and château, and had taken
the young girl with her.   They returned
after nightfall surrounded by servants with
torches.   I remember the steep roads, the
swaying of the great pine branches in the
wind, the moaning of the coming storm.
We reached the vast, rambling château in
safety.

'The Count had been supping alone.
He was excited beyond his wont.   The
Countess was fatigued and went to her

rooms at once. In one of the saloons of the château these two met.

'For one moment of wild delirium, for it was not pleasure, she gave up all. All the heaven of purity and peace and loving devotion and respect, all the innocent gaiety that was so happy because it was ignorant of conscious evil, all the memory of the past that was so lovely, all the hope of the future that was so bright, all that makes woman the priceless treasure of humanity, the beloved of Heaven! O, my God! My God!'

The Abbess stopped. De Brie sank from off his seat upon his knees and buried his face in his hands. There followed a silence that might be felt.

'It was only for a moment. Then she

tore herself from the Count's embrace and
fled, as with the brand of Cain, through
corridor and chamber. She threw herself
upon her bed, but long before the dawn
she rose, made her way to a familiar postern door, and went out into the night.

'The predicted storm had come, but
without rain. A brilliant, star-strewn sky
was overhead, a wild storm-wind swept up
the valley from the south and rent and
swung the great branches of the trees—the
great black branches that hung like ghostly
forms above my head. A terrible cry and
wailing, as of souls in torment, tore the distracted air and the distraught brain alike.

'Through the terraces of the garden,
over the strewn rack of leaf and flower
and branch, out into the wild forest; up

I

into the wooded dingles, not knowing, not caring whither she went, the girl hurried on, driven by remorse and by despair. At last she found herself on the borders of a great lake, a lake which she knew well. · It lay still and unruffled beneath the great rocks and the forests of pines and of oaks, undisturbed by the storm-tossed woodlands and howling, piercing wind, its unfathomable depths—in which, as legends reported, monsters of the prim-eval world still lurked—black and desolate beneath the starry, placid sky. Then long streaks of light, which were not those of the stars, began to draw themselves out beyond the mountains and the trees ; black clouds, flying as from a pitiless foe, hurried across the sky, torn and twisted into fan-

tastic shapes, and tinged here and there
with this strange, lurid light that was
coming into the sky: and above—far
above, out of all reach of human hope—
cold and icy and pitiless in the terrible
light, rose the great peak, white with the
starlight that was passing away, tinged, as
were the rushing storm-clouds, with the
glimmer of the dawn.

'On the bank of the cold, relentless
lake, dark with unknown horrors, the girl
stood at last. I believe now — I have
believed for years — that had she gone
back, the Countess, merciful, holy, forgiv-
ing as a saint, would have received her as
a daughter — that the Count would have
married her; but how could she go back?
How could she look into that loved face?

How could she stand before the gaze of those pure, those pitiful, those searching eyes?   How could she have married him? How could she have endured to live with him after that terrible, that fatal night?'

'She stood for a long time upon the waters' brink.   Some impulse, doubtless of God—for why should He who cares for the sparrows be supposed careless of this poor, distraught, maddened creature — restrained her from plunging into their solemn depths.   Suddenly a new thought, a flash of light — I do not think that it was of God — broke upon her mind, and brought with it something that resembled a dreary hope.   She would leave something that would be recognised as hers upon the grassy bank.   They would think that she had perished beneath the black, cold waters. They would forget her, or, perhaps, who could tell? when the first shock of disappointment and of loathing was over they might even pity her; and she, the Countess, she who was so loving and so merciful and so good, might even, in the pure summer dawns as she lay awake, might think of this poor child whom she had loved and befriended and lavished such gifts upon; and even as the years went on she might, who knows? think of her with something of the old love again —still as she would lie beneath the cold, black water, harmless and impotent to injure or to degrade her beloved son—remembering, as she surely would, how the girl had loved her, how sincere was her gratitude,

how true and devoted her love.   The girl
left her cloak and hat upon the bank, and
went on through the valley down into the
pass.

'For days and days she wandered on,
weary and half-starved, her feet torn and
bleeding by the roughness of the way,
begging for bread at the cottage doors.
Finally, after many days, she reached the
plains of Savoy.   At the first village of any
size that she reached, she sought a convent of nuns, she neither knew nor cared
of what order.   There she threw herself
upon the doorstep and lay as dead.'

WHEN the Countess awoke early in the spring morning, after a restless and uneasy sleep, the sunshine was flooding the room with warmth and light. She drank her morning cup of coffee, and when she was dressed she wandered out into the private garden alone in the pure, delicate air, driven by a devouring restlessness, a desperate insurrection against fate—against the life that seemed to be opening before her — against this terrible mistake which, as it seemed to her every moment more clearly, she had made—against this marriage

that would blot out all the possibilities of
joy during the few short years given her
of youth and beauty, and of the possibility
to enjoy. She paced up and down the
sunny terrace shaded by the yew hedges
like a beautiful, wild animal snared and
imprisoned by a cruel guile. The warm
sunshine, the fresh morning air laden with
the scent of opening blossoms, seemed to
quicken within her spirit a consciousness
of pleasure and an instinct of hope; with
the warm, scent-laden air there seemed to
glide into her sense, to thrill through every
nerve and vein, a personal and direct influence, *prévenant* and ingratiating, which
soothed her restless despair.

'Console yourself,' a suave, bland voice
seemed to whisper in her ear; 'your friend

will soon be here.   Your pleasant, kindly friend.'

Life seemed to open again before her with a prospect fair and alluring as a child's happy dream ; a waft of peace and easy indulgence, dear to human frailty, whispered compassion and allowance to her senses and in her ear.

.   .   .   .   .

When la Valliere awoke on the same morning his first thought was of his friend. The next was one of bewilderment and perplexity at the strange effect that the sight, as he supposed, of the Abbé had produced upon his friend.   What could he have seen that was so horrible, so terrible, as to deprive him of consciousness, and to produce, as the doctor had said, such a shock both to his body and his mind? He went to his friend's lodgings to inquire for him, but found that he had not returned from the convent, where he had passed the night. La Valliere went there, but failed to gain any information. The Abbess was fatigued and could not be seen. Monsieur de Brie, who appeared to be quite recovered, had left some time since, to go whither the portress did not know. La Valliere returned to his lodgings more perplexed and bewildered than when he had left them.

In the excited state of his feelings he naturally remembered the invitation of the Countess, with a desire to see again her beautiful face, to listen to her soft accents of kindly courtesy.

The distance between the city and the château was so short that la Valliere went there on foot.

The spring rain had laid every particle of dust, the morning was delicately fine, the birds sang in the parks and gardens that lay beside the road that stretched from the city gate in a straight line into the country. At first level, but beginning to undulate as it approached the hills, the road was planted on either side with rows of trees.

Before the young man had reached the confines of the Count's park he was conscious of a presence near him, and in another second the Abbé appeared to him, walking by his side, with an appearance of pleasant converse. There was now no necessity for effort, on la Valliere's part, before he could see or hear him; on the contrary, the intercourse seemed familiar and easy. Nevertheless, or perhaps even in consequence of such familiarity, la Valliere shrank from his companion with increased dislike.

'*Scélérat!*' he said excitedly; 'why do you dog my steps? What infernal spell did you cast yesterday night upon my friend? What did you do to him?'

And he laid his hand upon his sword.

'Gently, my son! gently!' said the other, always with his suave, masqued air and voice. 'You forget what I am. I did nothing to your friend. What he saw, he saw from no wish of mine, but by his own excited, fanatic imagination. Do not

let us speak of him or of any such fantastic
fools; other matters press upon our attention.   Do not slight the opportunity, the
moment that lies before you.   Be bold.
You will find the Countess in the private
garden.   Do not fear to be interrupted by
the Count.   I have taken care of him.'

'Wretch!' cried la Valliere; 'who!
what are you! that you should——?'

He spoke to the void air.   With a faint,
mocking smile the figure before him was
gone.

In the avenue that led up to the
château and in the straight walks of the
open garden that lay on either side, with
statues and long narrow canals of water
upon which swans were floating, several
people were walking, most of them, as la

Valliere knew, *notables* and persons of distinction in the city. They had come out to attend the *levée* of the Count, but he had not yet left his room, and the answers of the servants were vague and evasive. Several of these persons were known to la Valliere, and spoke to him; among them was the little Viscount.

'Ah, Monsieur la Valliere,' he said, as he came running up, his thin, elderly face wreathed with smiles, 'I see that you have followed my advice. You are a fortunate man. With that shape, that inimitable *tournure*, what may you not hope for?'

And he gazed with unfeigned admiration and envy at the handsome young actor.

'Have you seen Monsieur le Maire Carré?' he went on — 'I beg his pardon,

Monsieur Carré de Bois-Faucon—and con-
gratulated him on his nobility?'

'Is he noble?' said la Valliere, indifferently.

'Oh, surely. He has purchased the
office of Greyhounds of the King's Chamber, which gives nobility. His family dates
their nobility since exactly nine days. It is
perfectly correct. I have seen the receipt.'

La Valliere wished to shake him off,
but the little Viscount stuck to him.

'He will not, however, be able to join
in the assembly of the confraternity of
nobles which will take place in a few
days,' he said. 'None can do that who
cannot prove four quarterings. Your
friend de Brie might. He is noble of
far more than that. The de Bries of

Bois-Garou in Poitou, you know—wood-wolves they were, doubtless, in the old lawless days.'

La Valliere managed to escape from him after this, some other more important or responsive person attracting his attention. La Valliere spoke to the freshly-ennobled mayor, and to one or two other of the notables. There was a rumour current among them that the Count had left the château on some sudden and mysterious business.

At last the ancient major-domo appeared, and confirmed this report. 'The Count,' he said, 'had been suddenly called away to his lands at the Pic-Adam. Would *les messieurs* partake of *déjeûner* before returning to the city?'

'Les messieurs' would partake of *dé-jeûner*, and were marshalled into a dining-room on the ground floor of the château, facing the avenue and the public walks.   La Valliere seized the opportunity and spoke to one of the pages.   He in turn fetched a maid-servant, who, inspired by a bribe, spoke to the head woman of the Countess, who condescended to take his name to her mistress.   In a few moments an answer was returned.

'Madame la Comtesse would see Monsieur in the privy garden.'

The château was built in the taste of the latter part of the reign of Louis Quatorze, with sash doors and windows, at intervals in the façade, towards the private garden, opening on to a terrace

K

walk.   The windows and doors were
ornamented with carved stonework, pro-
fusely enriched with wreaths of flowers
and grotesque masques and grinning satyr
faces.

As, following the page, la Valliere
passed through several rooms, the air
seemed laden with an enervating perfume
and sultriness, as of a past luxury that
lingered in its ancient haunts ; outside, he
had left a mocking frivolousness, perhaps,
but a sense of fresh life and action—here,
in these scented, delicately pencilled, but
to some extent faded rooms, he seemed
to pass into another world, into an en-
chanted palace, a *Sans Souci* which extended before him wide as limitless desire.

'I have read,' he thought, 'somewhere

that "we are seekers after something in
the world, which is there in no satisfying
measure or not at all." It is not true.
The possibilities of existence are infinite.
Everything is possible to him who seeks!'

He passed out on to the long terrace
opposite to a flight of steps. Beneath
was a small lawn, screened by high yew
hedges, and by tall beech trees, cut into
regular and massive walls of interlaced
boughs. In the centre of the green, thus
enclosed from view even from the windows
of the château, were two fountains, springing from stone sculpture representing boys
holding dolphins, and between the fountains a solitary tall Arbor Vitæ reared its
green spire against the blue, spring sky.
Beside the Tree of Life, the flickering

sunlight through the fountain spray falling upon her, stood the Countess Eve.

She was dressed in a white morning robe of flowered silk, which clothed the faultless outline of her figure without concealing it by any monstrosities of fashion, and a white hat with an egret's plume looped with pearls. She smiled on la Valliere as he approached.

The sudden change from the heavy, scent-laden air of the luxurious rooms to the fresh, brilliant sunlight, the grotesque outlines and ornaments of the chambers, the château itself, with its architecture of carved faces amid wreaths of flowers, creeping serpents twined with roses and with jessamine, were, as it seemed, so many impresses and signatures of love.

He forgot the injunction, 'Let no man be hasty to taste of the fruit of Paradise before his time.' Whispering spirits, speaking to his soul, gave him courage and strength. A mystic veil of soft light, shining across his spirit, like the sunlit spray of the fountains across the Countess's figure, seemed to transform this lovely scene into the life of Fairy-land.

'I feared to venture into Paradise when at a distance, Madame la Comtesse,' he said. 'Now that I have been so bold, I wonder still more at my temerity. The bright reality, as I feared, appals and dazzles me.'

She looked at him simply and steadily out of her violet eyes.

'I asked you to come,' she said.

'There is no entrance into Paradise

without love,' thought la Valliere, but he did not utter the words.

'I was thinking of you this morning, Monsieur la Valliere,' the Countess went on, still speaking with perfect ease and simplicity, 'and of what you said the other night concerning the actor's life. I was wondering whether to you that which men call real was not altogether unimportant and frivolous, and whether the real to you was only the emotions and desires of the moment, and the characters and thoughts of those with whom you acted for a while; and I thought what a wonderful life this must be.'

She stopped and looked inquiringly at la Valliere, who thought he saw clearly what was passing through her mind.

'A wonderful life indeed,' he thought,
'she has glimpses of. Not the cruel, everyday round of dull and commonplace reality,
but the boundless choice of circumstance
and emotion ! What shall I tell her of such
a life ?'

It may seem an improbable thing, but,
though this was la Valliere's first and eager
thought, he was not able at once to express
it. At this most inopportune moment the
recollection of his friend de Brie, of what
his theory of life was and would have been,
forced itself upon his consciousness with
an insistence that would not be gainsaid.
It was as though de Brie stood by his side
—nay, forced himself between the Countess
and his friend.

It may have been that his actor's life

predisposed him to take at once the part of varied and opposing action, or it may have been that the influence of de Brie over his friend was so powerful that in absence even his spirit was by la Valliere's side.

However this may be, it is a fact that instead of the thought that was in his mind, or the purpose that had brought him thither, he spoke quite opposite words.

'My friend de Brie, Madame,' he said, 'would scold us both for entertaining such thoughts. He would preach us an edifying sermon on the necessity and certainty of facts, and of the duty of abiding by them, of neglecting the syren calls of the feelings and of the passions. I can see his attitude. I can hear his eloquent——'

La Valliere stopped in the midst of the

persiflage which his dual nature had at once awakened within him. The recollection of his friend's terror the night before, of his sudden faint and fall, arrested him. He faltered in his speech and turned pale ; then he stopped.

There was an embarrassed pause. The Countess seemed mystified and annoyed. The gracious smile left her lips, and the light seemed suddenly to fade from garden, alley, and lawn.

La Valliere bit his lip in vexation at what seemed to him his inexplicable stupidity. A dark shadow lay upon the path before him, which a moment before had seemed so bright, and, as out of a sudden thundercloud, the flash of a wielded sword intervened between himself and the Tree of Life.

But the shadow passed from the lovely face in another moment; la Valliere must have impressed the Countess's fancy to an uncommon degree.

'Your friend de Brie is no doubt a most excellent person,' she said archly, 'but I did not invite him here this morning. I do not know why he should intrude between us thus.'

They wandered on, after this, round the grassy verge of the fountains toward a flight of three broad steps, which led between the yew hedges to a long, broad terrace or alley, on a slightly lower level, extending the entire length of the garden. It was laid out in flower-beds of fantastic shapes upon the gravel paths. It was skirted on the upper or northern side by the high beech hedges, but on the southern side it was open to a wide lawn or orchard planted with fruit trees, and bounded on the lower side by the high ivy-grown wall that divided the private garden from the park, the lofty trees of which were seen towering above it.

The cherry and pear trees were bursting into blossom, the apple trees swelling into bud, the lofty trees in the park beyond showing the first faint green of the opening leaf, the bright spring sky stretched overhead. The Countess stood silently, looking over the white blossoms of the fruit trees towards the lofty branches of the park, through which might be seen here and there the white, rocky cliffs of the hills, and even, still

more remotely, the faintest outline of the
distant snowpeaks. A strange feeling of
confident boldness and strength came into
la Valliere's heart.

Never before had it seemed so clear to
him, standing in that bright spring morning by the side of this lovely woman,
that life—real life—did not consist in the
mere accidents of existence, in the limitations with which fact and circumstance
had cumbered the path of a man's life,
but in the limitless possibilities which his
imagination and his genius opened to him
on every side. 'Only,' as the whispering,
sardonic voice had said, 'only be bold.'

He was standing by the Countess's
side, a step backward behind her, by the
border of the grassy orchard.

'You are right,' he said, 'and de Brie is wrong. To love and to enjoy is the whole duty of man. The life which you have glimpses of is the only true existence —to rise above the confining limits of fact and circumstance—to dwell in the light and freedom of an untrammelled intellect, like to like, contrast to contrast, opposite to opposite. In this way life is raised to brilliancy and interest, as with a sparkling draught of sunlit elixir, that gives to all, even to the humblest, the heritage of the gods, and casts out all fear. "Ye shall not surely die."'

Did he speak these last words himself, or were they uttered by some unseen presence near him amid the garden walks? Some such fancy seemed to strike la Valliere, for he turned his head suddenly, but there was no one there.

The Countess did not seem to hear him. She kept her place, facing the white blossoms and the delicate sky. The flush of spring was in her face and in her eyes; but she did not speak.

There seemed, indeed, at this moment to fall upon the Countess and la Valliere one of those palls of silence that suddenly and without apparent cause embarrass us at times. We do not know the reason, we think of it only as an annoying stupidity, we blame ourselves. It is possible that we are wrong. It is possible that these sudden lets and hindrances are monitions of a higher life.

In the effluence of the Countess's look,

in the serenity and composure of her pose and gesture, there seemed some power to depress la Valliere's exultant spirits. He followed her a step or two behind, in silence.

Then, as they went on along the terrace towards the east, among the quaint borders edged with box, and turned down a path that skirted the lower lawn, and followed the high wall of the garden, la Valliere became conscious of the presence of another power; the air seemed to him full of something that could only be described as Effort, as supreme exertion of will towards a definite and determined end. He felt a strange certainty that the Abbé was by his side, and that the slightest exertion of his own will would cause him to be visible at the instant; but the presence and personality of the Countess absorbed his faculties and rendered such exertion impossible. The two wandered on in silence, hardly knowing what they did.

At the east corner, farthest from the château and from the city, the ground beyond the wall sloped suddenly into a small dingle, and this little valley was planted thickly with great trees that came close up to the wall, and even to the château itself. Near the corner of the wall, almost hidden by the heavy masses of untrained ivy, was a small postern door. Was it by chance or by some mysterious direction that, as la Vallière approached this door, he noticed it?

'That door,' he said, 'leads, I suppose, into the wood?'

'I suppose it does,' said the Countess, indifferently. 'It is never used. I believe it was made for the convenience of the Counts, that they might return to the privy garden and to the château unobserved. *Would you like to have a key?*'

Did she say these words herself? or were they spoken for her by some malefic power that was lurking near? She seemed to have some such thought as this, for she started as she said the words and looked round — furtively, if such a word might possibly be applied to her.

They walked round the grassy orchard

and returned to the château, where the *déjeûner* of the Countess awaited them. When, at midday, la Valliere left to return to the city, he took the key of the postern with him.

VIII

CLAUDE DE BRIE awoke on the morning
of this eventful day apparently restored
to perfect health. He went to mass at
the parish church adjoining the convent,
and after mass he had an interview with
the Abbess, as the result of which he
journeyed out to the château for the
purpose of seeing the Count. In this he
was unsuccessful; but being known to the
domestics at the château, he obtained
earlier news of the Count's sudden de-
parture than was vouchsafed to the
notables of the city. With this news he

returned to the Abbess, who manifested great perturbation on hearing it.

'He is driven by the devil into the wilderness,' she said; 'and in his despair there will be none to help him. Satan shall stand at his right hand. "Et diabolus stet a dextris ejus."'

The rule of the Abbess was not strict; she allowed the nuns to visit as they wished in the city and neighbourhood, but she herself never visited any on mere terms of civility or the customs of society. She spent her time, when not engaged in the management of her household, in visiting the poor in the city, or in such villages or farmhouses as she was by any means acquainted with. In this way it was not strange to her to take a sudden

journey on emergency. As she spoke
to de Brie, even, such a message was
brought to her from a neighbouring
village.

'Ah,' she said, 'poor child! she is very
lovely; she is the daughter of Monsieur
de Gesril. They are noble and live on
their own lands, but are very poor, and
the only sign of nobility is the *colombier*
at the farm; but I cannot think of her
now. I must go to him; I have delayed
too long.'

'I am at your service in all things,
my mother,' said de Brie; 'only command
me.'

'There are some people—good people
in their way,' said the Abbess, 'who have
an utterly unsubdued nature, which they

call God. May He grant that I have not been such a one! I have dreaded the pain of revealing myself to him. I have taken my own course and made my own fate. May God in His infinite pity have mercy upon me!'

'That,' said de Brie, below his breath, 'is the very prayer I heard the Count utter, as he thought of the moment when he might see you.'

'Our lives are interwoven in such mysterious sort,' said the Abbess, 'that we cannot always distinguish what the will of God is. I have heard of your mother's story. She was a child at a convent school. In this convent the Jansenist heresy obtained considerable sway. One of the nuns, who had great influence with this child, refused, among others, to submit to the ruling of the visiting Superior, and finally, with several more, broke her vow and left the convent. Your mother, who was completely under her influence, was about to follow her, when at this juncture your father appeared, married her, and carried her off. All this you know as well as I; but now, listen. This old nun, the other day, ninety years of age, being ill at ease, and for long desirous to return to her vocation, came back to us! Who can say where the hand of God is? I, like this old nun, chose my own path, hence this terrible growth of sin. Wherever there is sin committed, then sin is born into the world—is born, but does not die. Where

it wanders to, what work of evil is done
by it, none can tell. Driven to despair
by remorse, Satan standing at his right
hand, what may he not do? He who was
so gentle and so sweet-natured? Will
you go with me to his aid, Monsieur de
Brie?'

'*Ma mère*,' said de Brie, 'it seems to
me that God is more gracious to us than
we think. My mother, who, as you say,
left her convent partly through heresy and
partly through love, was discarded by all
her relations, by all her husband's relations
and friends. She seemed discarded by
God Himself. Her husband became a
common player and musician. But she
had contracted, in her convent, in spite of
heresy and in spite of love, a deep feeling

of religion and of absolute resignation to the will of God, which sustained her in life and supported her in death. She died happy. I, who am her son, owe everything that I have of happiness to her. I will go with you where you will.'

The Abbess looked at de Brie for some moments in silence. There could be no doubt that he was a happy man. His disposition was singularly sweet and placid, and he escaped, by an instinctive recoil, everything that was coarse, cruel, or unpleasant. His religion consisted in following the good and the beautiful, and he avoided intuitively the disquieting and difficult aspects both of life and thought. The existence of beauty was to him a safeguard and an asylum from all the attacks

of Satan and of doubt. It led him to a
Father in Heaven. To him the long
range of white summits were indeed the
heavenly Beulah. Every lovely chord, or
sunset, or mountain rill, or rocky valley,
assured him of a higher life ; and safe in
this fairyland, he could defy the distracting
sights of evil or the insinuating whispers of
doubt.

The impatience of the Abbess admitted
of no delay. At her urgent request de
Brie obtained a *chaise de poste*, and they
left the city that same afternoon, only a
few minutes, indeed, after la Vallière had
returned on foot from the château. The
Abbess was accompanied by an elderly
nun, in whom she placed confidence, and
who was much attached to her. De Brie

and a servant followed the chaise on horse-back.

They traversed the undulating plains, rich with woods and vineyards, that lay between the city and the hills. They slept at a little town at the foot of the mount-ains, in a romantic valley with a mountain torrent and lake, and mill-wheels that made a gentle, soothing murmur, and early in the morning dragged their way slowly up the long, steep road, beneath the lofty white rocks and the pine forests of the Jura range.

Snow still covered the tops of the hills, which were partially concealed by wreaths of delicate white vapour, drawn out and con-torted into fantastic and fleeting shapes, through which the sharp outlines and

weird forms of the pine forests were in-
distinctly traced.   Every few moments a
rift in the seething mist revealed a delicate
blue sky, and sudden bursts of sunshine
lighted the fresh green of the sycamore
and chestnut and beech woods.   A sudden light, climbing the steep hillsides,
revealed, now and again, the verdant pastures, and the delicate shimmer of spring
flowers on the grassy slopes and in the
fissures of the rocks.

Near the summit of the hills they
reached a churchyard, when, alighting and
looking back, they saw the mountain lake
and the winding valleys which they had
passed.   Then through a gorge of pine-
clad hills they reached Saint Cergne, and
then, immediately afterwards, without a

moment's warning, the road reaches the verge of the precipice, and the wall of the Jura opens right and left, and the finest view in the world bursts upon the traveller's gaze.

The writings of Rousseau had made the love of the picturesque in mountain scenery fashionable, but both the Abbess and de Brie would have paused before such a sight had Rousseau lived or not. The Abbess alighted from the *chaise de poste*, and de Brie dismounted and stood by her side.

At the distance of some eight miles, embossed upon a plain of verdure, of woodland, and of vineyard, there lay, or rather hovered before the sight, so delicate and shaded and ideal was the vision, the apparition, as it might seem, of a celestial lake. Of a colour deeper than that of the most fathomless sky, its margin indistinct with snow-white reflection, like the hovering of shadowy wings, it seemed, from where they stood, to rise above the earth as a pathway and pavement of that city whose foundations are sapphire; and above this marvellous and glorious sight there rose another more glorious and wonderful still, for above the pavement of this mystic sea rose into the sky, pure in a whiteness hitherto unconceived, distinct against the delicate morning light, piled in stupendous fashion, etched in lines of marvellous witchery and glamour, in pointed peak and giant strength, the stainless region of the snow.

.   .   .   .   .

The Abbess and de Brie stood 'some minutes in silence; but the heart of the Abbess was too full of one absorbing subject to permit of its being long distracted towards any other. She pointed out to de Brie, in the far distance towards the south, a peak of snow standing somewhat apart, white and phantom-like in the air.

'That is the Pic-Adam,' she said. 'We must skirt the mountains by Chambéry. The passes before us are closed at this time of the year, but by Chambéry we can reach the Pic by a lower pass. It will be a long journey. Pray God we do not come too late!'

.   .   .   .   .

On the evening of the third day the

chaise de poste, toiling slowly up the pass from Chambéry, reached the Château du Pic-Adam. It stood, with its dark massive masonry and projecting Gothic towers and upper windows, its pinnacles and lofty slop- ing roofs, surrounded by thick groves of oak and chestnut on the hillsides; and above it, high above the neighbouring pine- woods, rose the narrow snowpeak, the western sun shining full upon it. Over the château and below the peak, partly upon a low rain-cloud and partly upon the dark pinewood, a rainbow crossed the mountain slope.

'That is a good omen,' said de Brie, riding up close to the door of the chaise. 'We shall not be too late.'

The tired horses dragged the chaise

slowly up on to the broad terrace of the château, which was planted along the edge with a straight row of sycamore trees. From the farther end de Brie could see the peak, from which all trace of sunset had faded, and below it, at some distance from the terrace, the fatal lake. The rainbow was gone.

The solemn bell of the château sounded long and drearily in the deepening gloom before there was any response.

At last an old servant, accompanied by a youth in an old and worn livery, appeared, and jealously inspected the visitors through the partly open door.

The appearance and manner of de Brie succeeded in partly reassuring the old man, and he ventured forth as far as the chaise

door, where the Abbess spoke to him for a
few minutes in a low voice.

'*La mère Abbesse*,' he said, 'might certainly enter with her attendants.' He
seemed dazed and confounded.

The last faint glow of evening light
shone upon the great hall as they entered.
It was an immense apartment, longer than
it was broad, with a comparatively low
ceiling, crossed by gigantic beams of oak,
and running through the entire depth of
the house. On the right hand was an
enormous, carved, stone fireplace, of greater
length than height, and opposite to it a
collection of armour of all ages and descrip-
tions, both arranged upon the wall and
standing in front of it in entire suits. At
the back of the hall were two flights of

steps and a low square window full of dark-
stained glass, with armorial bearings in the
small panes.

Monsieur le Comte had been there,
said the old servant, since three days. He
believed that he was then in his room, but
he would inquire of his servant.

The young footman produced two
candles in lofty candlesticks and lighted
the Abbess and de Brie up the wide strag-
gling stairs. The wind moaned dismally
through the doors and windows and down
the pannelled walls, and caused the candles
to flicker and burn dimly. De Brie's
spirits sank amid the gloom.

'This house,' said the Abbess, 'seems to
you, I do not doubt, silent, empty and
deserted, but it is far otherwise with me.

To me it seems full of restless footsteps.
I see these rooms and stairs full of servants and dependants, and of guests. I
hear the talk and jests and laughter; I hear
Madame's voice. The air is full of voices
and of echoing footsteps. Those who have
lived and worked, and thronged the chambers of old ·houses — where are they?
Where are the absent and the dead?
Surely they are not far from us in such a
house as this is ?'

She walked straight on as if through
her own house. The staircase led to a
long gallery which stretched away on
either hand far beyond the distance to
which the faint light of the two candles
extended. It appeared to be lined, as
was the staircase, with dim and faded

portraits, and here and there with cabinets
and embroidered chairs, all equally ancient
and out of fashion.

The Abbess crossed the gallery, opened
a door, and entered a great saloon apparently over the hall, and the young
servant followed her submissively.

The *salle* was furnished much in the
same fashion as the rest of the house.   If
there had ever been in it anything modern
or elegant, it had long since been removed.
Everything wore that look of oneness, that
sameness of tint, that attaches itself to furniture which has been long in the same place.

The Abbess crossed the *salle* and
opened a door on the further side.   By
this door, where a picture had formerly
hung, there was a blank space.

'She used to be there,' said the Abbess.
'The Count has the picture at the
château.'

They went through several smaller
rooms, all furnished in the same way, all
bearing the same marks of desertion and
emptiness.   Finally they reached a door,
which seemed to end the suite.   Here the
Abbess paused for a moment with her hand
upon the lock.   Then she opened the door
and went in.

The room had a more modern appearance than any that they had yet seen. It was
a bedroom of considerable size, furnished
in the taste of the Louis Quatorze period
of thirty years before.   The embroidered
bed-hangings, the marqueterie wardrobes,
the *garniture de toilette* and little tables,

were undisturbed — left exactly as their mistress had left them years ago. The room was carefully kept, and some repairs had been made where the hangings and covers had become worn and rotten with age.

'This was Madame's room,' the Abbess said; but de Brie had known it already.

In this room, as in every room of the house, was the sense of unseen presences of the absent and of the dead, of a people and of owners who had passed away, and to whom everything still belonged. It seemed incredible that any should dare to alter or to touch. All such meddling would seem intrusion and wrong—wrong to the past and to the dead.

The Abbess crossed the room and stood

before a large wardrobe of rich marqueterie, the upper part opening with doors,
the lower consisting of drawers. One of
these—the upper one—the Abbess opened.

'Here,' she said, as she drew it out,
'she kept her own jewels, her most cher-
ished——' with a sharp cry she sank upon
her knees, and covering her face with her
hands, burst into a passion of tears.

In the drawer, carefully folded and
preserved as with the hand of love, strewn
with the withered remnants of what had
once been sweet-smelling flowers and
herbs, with here and there a girl's orna-
ment and jewel, were the dresses of a
young girl of the passed fashion of perhaps
some twenty years.

*   *   *   *   *

In a few moments the steps of the old major-domo were heard. The Abbess rose from her knees and recovered her self-possession.

'Monsieur le Comte's servant informed him,' the old man said, 'that his master had retired to his room, and had dismissed him with orders that he was not to be disturbed until a certain hour in the morning. He dared not disobey his orders. If *la Mère Abbesse* and monsieur would partake of some supper, such refreshment as the house afforded was at their service. In the morning the Count's will could be ascertained.'

There was no alternative but to submit to the delay.

A lovely morning, foretold by the rainbow which had attracted de Brie's regard
the evening before, dawned upon the
château, the valley, and the peak.   Before
his servants were awake, the Count rose and
wandered out through the terraced garden
and the fresh green woods towards the
margin of the lake, whose dark waters had
so terrible an attraction to him.   Twenty
years ago, on a wild tumultuous morning,
he had stood almost on the same spot, his
mind distracted with remorse and despair.
Since then there had been seasons, long
seasons, when the terror and the despair, and
even the past itself had been almost, if not
quite, forgotten ; but beneath all the asso-
ciations and the preoccupations, the dis-
tinctions and the successes of his life, had

lurked a germ of conscious memory and
of remorse. Whether aroused by return
to scenes of his boyhood, or by the
presence of his lovely wife, the remembrance of this other girl—none less lovely
—the companion of his boyhood, the love·
and fancy of his youth, dogged his steps
from day to day. Fanned, as it would
seem, for their own malefic purpose, by
the spirits that track the footsteps of the
sinner, the remembrance became to him
in itself a sin. By a terrible action and
reaction, committed sin had become not
only exceeding sinful, but a diabolic witch-
circle without exit and without end.

Yet, though he stood on that lovely
morning by the grassy margin of the lake,
himself as remorseful and despairing as

when he had stood there twenty years
before, how changed otherwise was the
scene! *Then*, on the stormy autumn
morning, the great sere and withered
leaves, swept and driven through the air
and along the earth, hurled and contorted
into fantastic shapes and measures like
the witch - dances of a Walpurgis night;
then, the gigantic branches of the forest
trees, torn and riven and hurled and
strewn upon pathway and rock and green
sward; *then*, the roar and wail as of the
storm - fiend through mountain pass and
pine wood; *then*, the storm-clouds hunted
and driven across the affrighted sky.
Now, along the margin of the lake, upon
the green, fresh - springing turf, hyacinth
and crocus and anemone, countless in

number, spread out a carpet fit for the dancing of the summer hours; *now*, the laughing waters of the lake, just stirred by the morning breeze, flashed with opal tints of blue and gold beneath the newly risen sun, and above, over the gay, rustling wood, loud with the singing of birds, the Pic - Adam, cold, clear, steadfast, in the sky.

The Count was standing, his hands crossed behind his back, his head bent forward upon his chest, as nearly as he or any man might be able to judge, precisely on the spot where, twenty sad years before, a girl's hat and scarf had been found soiled and torn upon the rotted turf.

A slight noise caused the Count to turn

suddenly and sharply round, and he saw
de Brie, whom he remembered with in-
distinctness.   He instinctively laid his
hand upon his sword.   De Brie was
standing hesitatingly upon the flowery
grass.   He was very pale, and his manner
was embarrassed and almost timid.   The
Count looked at him with wonder and
even alarm.

'Pardon me, Monsieur le Comte du
Pic-Adam,' said the young man at last,
'that I intrude upon your seclusion.   I
have a message, I may say, from the
grave.'

He spoke slowly as if to gain time.
He was indeed overpowered by a sense
of nervousness, and scarcely knew what
he said.   Even with his knowledge of the

past—of what the past day, the past hour
had brought—a strange sense of mystery
and uncertainty haunted him. What
was about to happen he could not tell.
Nothing that might happen would seem
strange.

The Count looked at him very steadily,
but he did not take his hand from his
sword.

'Monsieur le Comte,' de Brie went on,
still speaking very slowly, 'we are not
alone. We are never alone; we are
surrounded by the living and the dead,
here with us one moment and then gone
for ever; and not only by such but by
those others who never die. Do you
believe this?'

The supreme distinction of face and

gesture, the tone of his voice, were so perfectly noble and innocent of evil, that all trace of suspicion and doubt vanished from the Count's look.   He took his hand from his sword.

'I believe it,' he said; 'no one has reason to know it better than I.'

'"She must be ever near me, ever near me, and yet I never see her,"' de Brie went on.   'Monsieur le Comte, do you remember using these words?'

'When I see her!' exclaimed the Count; 'when I see her!'   In his eyes the dazzling lake, the waving woodland, the green sward covered with flowers, seemed only a fitting stage for this distinguished mysterious stranger, who spoke such penetrating words.   He felt almost like those priests of old, who saw, in the ministrations of their course, angels by the altar of the Lord. 'When I see her! May God in His infinite pity have mercy on me when I do!'

As he said these words, de Brie saw a strange light come into his eyes, as he stood with his back to the lake, facing de Brie and the château, whence the young man had come. De Brie turned suddenly, and the Count's surprise was, perhaps, hardly greater than his own.

Within the shadow of the wood, where the grassy verge began to drop towards the lake, stood a figure more like an angel of God than falls to the lot of most men, in their course through life, ever to see.

The white lining of the Abbess's dress

N

was thrown back, and hung like folded
wings on either side of her slight, noble
figure, clothed in what seemed the rich
dress of a young girl of a past age ; on her
breast an antique gem flashed in the morning light.   Her closely-cut hair, released
from all covering, seemed to surround her
head with a halo of glory, shot through by
the sun.   De Brie gazed upon her with
wonder and with awe.   The Count sank
upon his knees.

'Auguste,' she said, and the lingering
air seemed to caress and to prolong the
sound ; 'Auguste, I am here.   I have
never seen you since that night, but I am
here.   God in His unspeakable pity has
had mercy upon us, and has utterly abolished the whole *body* of Sin.'

THE key which the Countess Eve had
given to la Valliere made the entrance into
Paradise very easy to him. He came day
after day, at the same hour in the morning,
to the postern door in the wood. He
hired a horse, upon which he made a
circuit of a few miles every morning, and
leaving his horse at a farm and game-
keeper's house in the little valley, he made
his way to the private door through the
wooded paths. Every day the spring sunshine seemed brighter, and every day the
sky above him seemed more blue. Every

day the budding leaves grew greener, and
the fruit blossom more white and dazzling
against the blue sky. The rich moulding
of masques and flowers and fruit that
shone out amid the trellised trees in the
renaissance work of the château seemed
to glow with welcome in the warmth of
their mellow, moss-tinted colouring, and
morning after morning, beneath the fountains and the Tree of Life, without fail to
receive him, stood the Countess Eve.

'It is good of you to come,' she said;
'you are the truest of friends, for you are
never late.'

Do you wish me to tell you what they
said? Do you ask me what the rushing
brooklet is saying when the tiny waves
ripple and sparkle in the light? Do you

think that I can crystallise the warmth and
the glow and the sunlight, the flush of
youth and the fresh breeze of life and of
the spring ? — the bounding spirits, the
health and vigour of the warm life within
the bud ? Were I able, by some, magic
science, to trace in sound to your ears
every syllable that fell from their lips,
would you be aught the wiser ? Would
you be nearer, if you have it not without,
to a perception of what these two felt and
enjoyed ? Was the talk so brilliant, do
you suppose ? Was it couched in the antithesis and epigram that look so clever in
print ? In the Paradise to which you look
back with a fond remembrance, was your
talk so brilliant ? Would it have stood
the ordeal that demands such sparkling

dialogue in the novels of the day? and, if not, why should you demand it of la Valliere and the Countess Eve?

But there was, it must be owned, something in the nature of things which, though untranslatable into English talk, yet should not be altogether forgotten. In the sparkling, clear air, untainted by the foulness of smoke, or impurity of stagnant mist,—a sparkling freshness peculiar to France,—in the ravishing connection of blue sky and white blossom, and the delicate green tracery of spray of bursting leaf, with the yellow, moss-tinged, carved work of the Château, with grinning satyr heads and friezes of wild, dancing figures turned to stone, was something so *germain* to the light, sparkling nature of the old French world—so truly, at the same time, the author and the offspring of it—that it is not given, without an effort, to the northern, slumberous imagination to see these things as they really were, to understand either the scene or the people of these places, or of these reckless, brilliant hours.

To la Valliere, indeed, it seemed as though he were translated into an ethereal region, left alone to be driven hither and thither by his own unbridled will and desire. De Bric seemed to have deserted him, vanished unaccountably from the scene at the very moment when his distinct personality and powerful influence over his friend might have been thought most needed. All help seemed to be denied to him. The ways and effects of evil—of committed sin—are too varied to be foreseen or guarded against.

.   .   .   .   .

The fifth day after de Brie had so mysteriously disappeared was a Sunday, and la Valliere did not take his accustomed ride that morning. He had some reason to expect that the Countess would attend High Mass at the cathedral of the city —at any rate he strolled into that service in the middle of the morning.

The cathedral was full of worshippers when la Valliere entered it. He had come in from idleness and curiosity more than from any other motive, and wandered round the outskirts of the congregation by the great western door. He entertained himself by observing the demeanour and differing classes of the worshippers. They were of both sexes and of all ages, and of that class which, in Catholic countries, hovers on the borders of the Church, not exactly wishing to break with it, but in no way submitting to its rule. It consisted for the most part of men, some of whom were young men, and a few women of the lowest class; their more decent sisters were higher up in the vast nave.

A vista of pillars of immense size and towering height, carved and ornamented at the top to the depth of many feet, struck la Valliere's gaze as he entered. Beyond, far beyond, high in the misty, distant roof, a gigantic crucifix crowned, with a vague, mysterious awe, a screen of wonderfully elaborate stonework, relieved by tier above tier of the dark mahogany of pulpit stair and gallery and pinnacle, and of the carved fretwork of the stalls.   Beyond, still beyond, rapt away from human touch or intrusion as it seemed, at least to these distant loiterers, remote from human sense, a region of transcendental mystery and glory, from which, partly hidden by cloud-wreaths of incense and by the guardian screens, and even by the crucifix, was dimly present to the sense and feeling the unspeakable awe of white altar and pix and sacrament.

La Valliere found himself standing by a young man of more intelligent and refined aspect than most of those about him, evidently a workman in some delicate art.

He was looking round upon the people, most of whom were kneeling, with an expression of contempt.

'What brings all these people here?' he said aloud, but possibly only to himself.

'What brings them here?' said la Valliere. 'What brings you here?'

'The music partly,' said the young man, not so much to la Valliere as in answer to some thought of his own; 'then hunger, and because I have nothing else to do.'

La Valliere gazed at him curiously, but before he could answer there was a sudden hush in the wave of sound, and an intenser sense of awe and worship swept over the kneeling crowd and reached even to the outcasts and mockers and indifferent that had wandered within the limits of the sacred fold, round the precincts of the western door. Far away, surrounded and guarded by hierarchies and priests and reverent worshippers, the Ineffable Presence was revealed; but amid the hushed stillness there fell upon the ear the passing of gentle footsteps, as two priests, followed by serving brothers carrying baskets of loaves, distributed, to whosoever would receive them, pieces of consecrated bread, remembering, surely, One who, amid a desert wild of Galilee, had compassion on the multitude, 'because they had come from far, and had nothing to eat.'

'Will you take it?' said the young man to la Valliere, with a still more bitter sneer. 'It is not for food. It is an obsolete, superstitious charm—doubtless of great virtue, but to enjoy it you must kneel to a priest!'

La Valliere looked at him again. There was a bitter, desperate look in the young man's eyes that he did not like. La Valliere was not the man to involve himself in any trouble or inconvenience that might be avoided by a prudent indifference. He turned and left the cathedral. He did not take the sacred bread.

.   .   .   .   .

As he came out into the then hushed and quiet market-place, soon, as the day drew on, to be the scene of gaiety and noise, the devil entered into la Valliere, as surely as he entered into Judas Iscariot, though he himself was perhaps unconscious of it, and no outward sign revealed the fact.

In the city market-place and through
the empty streets, as often in the pathways
of the sunny wood, stealthy footsteps
seemed to echo and to keep pace with his
own ; the bland, suggestive voice which by
this time he knew so well, whispered,
'You have attained to so much, surely you
are not satisfied. Only be bold! Nothing
is possible to those who fear—impossible
to the courageous and the bold.'

And, indeed, la Valliere was stifled
and constrained within the solemn, stately
walks and shaded alleys of this decorous,
princely garden—a type, as it might well
be thought, of what reserved and virtuous
life might seem to him to be. The very
beauty of such a life oppressed him. It
was to him as though the very dust and

stain of daily, reckless life, with all the
sorrow and the soil which such a life
may bring—will surely bring—was to be
chosen before such a decorous, decent life
as this, surrounded and protected as it was
by this stateliness, this beauty and refinement; the loveliness of the Countess even
seemed to lose something of its charm.
She was still above him and out of his
sphere. A wild, degraded, selfish desire
took possession of him, a passionate longing to see her elsewhere, in common, vulgar
life, amid sordid and tawdry surroundings,
and people far beneath her, of whose existence she had hitherto perhaps scarcely
dreamed; to bring her down to his level,
nay, beneath it; to possess her with the
friendly familiarity which such a life allows.

The adventures and scenes in which, night after night, he took his part upon the stage, suggested to him incidents and embarrassing situations without number. He fancied this lovely, stately creature involved in such situations and scenes. His imagination revelled in them with an ever-increasing zest. In every such scene his own lower nature played a principal part, found a sensual and an unclean gratification. Satan stood at his right hand.

. . . . .

The next morning he was standing, as usual, by the Countess's side, in Paradise, in the centre of the long alley, fronting the white flowering blossoms and the green ranges of the wood.

'Your life is crippled and confined,' he

said suddenly, 'with all this pomp and solemn decorum. You do not know what life is; how bright and cheerful, and full of zest and interest and humour and fun. You have no perception of the contrast that gives pleasure to the free, gay, reckless life of shine and shade, of storm and calm, of hunger and feasting, of quarrellings and makings-up. For myself, this life would suffocate me. Could you taste, but for an hour, the other life, you would never return to this.'

Why did the light seem to fade from glade and garden alley in the Countess's eyes as she looked up the stately walk on either hand?

'I shall go into the city this afternoon,' she said in a soft tone; 'it is very stupid, but it seems to me that I see life. I shall go to a fête *chez Monsieur le Maire.* There will be dancing on the trellised lawns, and music. Then I shall go to the vesper service. Every one is there, and there is much talk, but it is always the same—the same badinage, the same jokes, that stupid little Vicomte with his spiteful stories. It is very dull,'—and the Countess sighed—'but surely I see life.'

La Valliere smiled—the sort of superior smile of an inferior nature.

'That is not the life I speak of, Countess,' he said. 'You noble ladies know nothing of life. Did you ever wonder why it was that your nobles—your husbands and your brothers—spend so much of their time away from you? Did it ever occur to you—do you not see—that it is that they may enjoy something of this free life, something of this tattered, soiled striving with fate—this life which is not shackled by the bonds of wealth and custom, but which knows something of the joys of poverty and of reckless existence from day to day, upon what the day's successes—or the day's failures, for that matter—may bring? I would it were possible for me to show you something of this life.'

The Countess turned her face toward la Valliere and looked him full in the eyes. There was a flushed colour in her cheeks and an inquiring, searching look in her eyes that would have been trying for some men to face, thinking the thoughts that he was thinking, yet he stood it without flinching.

The pseudo-art in which he was a proficient absorbed his whole faculties in the project of the moment, the success of which became to him, for the time, the sole important aim in life. If the part were well played—if the character, whatever it were, was well maintained throughout—it mattered nothing how it stood with regard to a moral law, to the wellbeing of those with whom it had to do. The spirit of a born actor possessed him. As this lovely creature fixed her eyes upon his he felt as though a power that was not his own gave him confidence and strength. She was—in spite of the soft loveliness of her face and expression, and of the rounded

outline of her form—of that stately and
commanding stature and beauty, of that
fulness and perfection of figure, of that
steadiness and gravity of look, that makes
woman not the frail suppliant for man's
pity and protection, but his equal and com-
petitor in the race of life—a fact that adds
to the enterprise, in the eyes of many men,
an unspeakable zest, that makes such a
woman a priceless possession, an exquisite
prize.

It was a strange and terrible thing, but,
as she looked at him, he seemed to grow
in beauty and in power. A fascination of
which she had been unconscious hitherto
seemed to issue from his look and figure,
as though some glamour from below—it
could hardly have come from heaven—had

been suffused into him by deadly magic
and guile. A fatal, alluring attraction
seemed to overmaster her will, to lure
and to induce her to waver in her lofty
calm, to throw down her highborn reserve, to follow him even to poverty and
to shame.

And, indeed, there was in la Valliere's
expression and countenance something that
might well lure and persuade the will, in
the perfectly-cut features, the delicate, distinct eyebrows, the thin, suasive lines of the
mouth, closed but trembling as it were in
the act to open with dulcet sound, in the
full and confident yet inoffensive gaze of
the almond-shaped, finely-shaded eyes, a
gaze full of conscious sympathy, of a wide,
all-embracing perception and knowledge

and friendliness. A beautiful, persuasive creature, strangely in touch and keeping with the soft beauty and peace of the garden which it seemed fated to annul and to destroy.

'Shall I not trust this man?' thought the Countess Eve. 'Shall not I, too, see something of this life of which he speaks, I feel, so well? Why should not women also know something of good and evil? Where is my husband at the present moment? If he may leave his home and wander over the face of the earth in search of adventures, surely so may I.'

It must have been some demon that put this thought into her mind just then.

'What do you want me to do?' she said.

' I will have two horses in the valley
outside the postern door at this time to-
morrow,' said la Valliere, hardly knowing
indeed what he said, so entirely did the
words seem prompted to him. ' Come
masqued. Many ladies wear masques to
protect their faces from the dust. We can
return the same way.'

' I will come,' she said.

.   .   .   .   .

Each morning in that fair springtime
rose, if it might be, more lovely than the
last. Every gift that could make earth
or life attractive seemed lavished upon
sky and land. A mild, soft night had
caused the spring to burst almost into full
summer in a few hours, and had bathed
all the fresh wood and the grass and

flowers with a sparkling crystal veil' of pearly light and mist.

The Countess came into the garden at the appointed hour and passed down to the postern door, her masque in her hand.

There was no tremor in the blue sky over her head, no sudden pallor on the golden flowers of the earth, no warning note or stillness in the choir of birds that filled the air with music. The Countess put the key into the lock. It grated harshly as she turned it, but it turned easily to her hand. It had been turned often of late. She opened the door and went out.

The light lay clear upon the grassy turf and on the stems of the great trees dappled with sunshine and with shade; her heart stopped with a sudden shock and stillness, for; the moment that she passed the threshold, she saw It for the first time.

It was only for a second. All the power of hell, all the glamour and delusion and sorcery at the command of the Prince of Evil, were exerted at the moment to recall the false step, to cancel the sight; but it was too late. She had seen, by the power and light of God's conscience in a pure spirit—she had seen, at the moment of a fatal error, the face of committed Sin.

What she saw she never knew. The horror of the sight, whatever it was, blasted her memory, and left it so far a ghastly blank. She sank upon her knees before the still open door of Paradise, her face buried in her hands.

THE same day that la Valliere had left the Countess, he acted at night in the little theatre in the city. In no crisis of his fate, however severe, would he willingly have kept away from the stage or renounced his part.

Here and there, in other nations, have individuals felt this unique attraction for the stage ; but in no nation, as to the French, has been given such ability, delicacy, and perfection in the representation of every aspect which character can assume or which incident can furnish. Act-

ing and the stage, in France or among
Frenchmen, is a different thing, altogether
a distinct art and place, from the craft and
the boards which are called by these names
in other countries.   In the possession of
this gift la Valliere was a true French-
man.

When he came off the stage, instead of
finding, as he usually did, his friend de
Brie waiting for him, he was accosted by
the little Viscount.

'Monsieur la Valliere,' he said, 'you
have been perfectly charming to-night; you
have surpassed yourself.   Might I hope
that you will condescend to sup with me
to-night?'

They went out into the moonlit streets,
accompanied by a boy carrying a torch.

In a silent and somewhat deserted street, in a part of the city which had once been fashionable at a time when centralisation had not crushed out all provincial life in France, they stopped at the *portière* of a large and apparently luxurious house. The great door falling back, they found themselves in a passage, which was chiefly lighted by the large fire of a porter's lodge on one side. From the lodge, where apparently he had been warming himself before his fire, there appeared a valet or serving-man, of the true old French type.

'Ah! la Fleur,' said the Viscount, 'I hope you have something presentable for supper. I have brought with me a most distinguished gentleman, whom probably you know very well by sight.'

La Fleur bowed with a complaisant smile. 'It would distress me,' he said, 'were Monsieur le Vicomte badly served, whether he returns alone or with company.'

They followed la Fleur and the boy, who had procured candles instead of his torch, up a large and somewhat imposing staircase. As they ascended, la Valliere soon perceived that they were not the only inhabitants of the house. Sounds of talking and even of quarrelling were heard, and figures, some of them in decided dishabille, peeped at them round corners and flitted from their sight down passages. They were conducted into a comfortably but antiquely-furnished dining-room, where a round table was set for supper.

The Viscount showed la Valliere into an adjoining room, and begged to be excused for a few moments. When la Valliere came out into the supper-room the Viscount was entering with two large and dusty bottles of wine in his hands. He welcomed la Valliere again with enthusiasm.

'Monsieur,' he said, 'it gives me the sincerest pleasure to entertain you. You have given me, I say it from my heart, some of the most delightful moments that have occurred in a life that has been by no means too full of pleasure. I give you in return what I have.'

La Valliere was touched by the little man's evident sincerity. He expressed himself as politely as he could.

'You may be surprised,' continued the Viscount, 'to find me in so large a house. That is easily explained. When my family gave up *la vie de province* and lived entirely in Paris, they resigned to me this house—their town house—as my portion. You may have wondered, sometimes, why I remain here at all, and do not go to Paris. That is a long story which need not be told here. I began life as a page to the Queen. When I left the pages I entered the marine, which I did not like. *Voilà tout.* I entered into a compact with la Fleur. He lets the house. I reserve for myself two or three rooms. You may have noticed, even since you have been here to-night, that there are other inmates.'

La Valliere admitted that he had.

'Yes,' continued the Viscount, 'there are complications, at times disturbances; but it is life, it is entertaining—at times very much so.   Besides it is remunerative. Ah! here is supper.'

La Fleur entered, accompanied by the boy, and supper was served.   It consisted of small carp from the river, in a great dish, a *poulet* delicately cooked with truffles, and other dainties, all exquisitely served.

'This *carpillon*,' said the Viscount, 'at this time of year, caught in certain reaches of the river, is considered very fine.'

'It is delicious,' said la Valliere.

As he spoke la Fleur filled the glasses from one of the bottles the Viscount had himself brought up.

La Valliere had taken part of his glass, when he put it down suddenly, and looked at the Viscount inquiringly.

' Ah !' said the other, evidently pleased, ' you like that wine. That is good. I like a man who knows what he is drinking. There is a somewhat curious story about that wine. When my family gave up this house as a city house, they took away most of the furniture to Paris ; but there was some wine left, and la Fleur and I used to visit the cellars.'

' If the wine they left,' said la Valliere, emptying his glass, which la Fleur had refilled in the meantime, ' was of this quality, it speaks more for their complaisance than for their taste.'

The Viscount smiled. ' Listen,' he

said. ' By and by—we used to visit the cellar, la Fleur and I——'

La Fleur, who must have heard the story often, was standing by with a reserved, amused air.

' La Fleur and I.   Suddenly, one day, we perceived a door which neither of us had before observed.   We tried to open it. It resisted our efforts, although the lock was broken off.   We forced off a portion of the rotted wood.   Then we perceived that the whole vault, or small cellar, was filled with a huge fungus, which prevented the door from opening inwards.   We cut it out piecemeal with an axe.   Then at the back we discover a small *réduit* of this wine.   *Voilà!*   It must have been there a century—who knows ? '

La Fleur filled the glasses again.

'I only produce this wine,' said the Viscount, 'for my most especial friends. I have already said that I am under most peculiar obligation to you. La Fleur respects my secret.'

'Monsieur le Vicomte,' said la Fleur, breaking silence at last in a soft voice, 'has attached himself to me by so many acts of condescension and kindness that it would be infamous were I to betray his slightest confidence.'

'Wine,' said the Viscount, 'is a wonderful thing. I have read in an old book that belonged to a great-uncle of mine, who was a great *curioso*—a book written by an English doctor to that king of theirs whose head they cut off; funny thing, was it not, to cut off a king's head? but the English are naturally eccentric—this doctor, partly out of his own head, and out of van Helmont and Paracelsus, tells strange things, of strifes and histories, that go on within the nature of wine, until the perfect spirit is born, and is purified, and escapes, and triumphs over gorgons and demons and slaves, and becomes immortal and the giver of immortality. All this had something to do with the existence of that mystic fungus that filled that cellar of ours — which fills other cellars, as I have heard. It certainly is wonderful wine.'

And with a voice somewhat cracked, but in which much of the old sweetness yet lingered, he sang Sganarelle's air—

' Qu'ils sont doux
Bouteille jolie,
Qu'ils sont doux,
Vos petits glougloux !
Mais mon sort ferait bien des jaloux,
Si vous étiez toujours remplie.
Ah ! bouteille, ma vie,
Pourquoi vous videz-vous ?'

When they had dispatched the *poulet aux truffes*, and la Fleur had served an omelette and other delicacies, he left the room, and the two men were left alone. La Valliere was seized with a sudden idea, inspired probably by the wine.

' Monsieur le Vicomte,' he said, ' I wish you would add another to the favours you have already granted me by asking me to *déjeûner* to-morrow and allowing me to bring a friend ? '

The Viscount looked at him with surprise.

' And this friend ? '

' Is the Countess Eve.'

' Mon Dieu ! ' cried the Viscount, ' you
have not lost time ! And, pray, what
should the Countess Eve do here ? '

' I have promised the Countess,' said
la Valliere, ' that she should see life. It
strikes me that in your *ménage*, from what
you have told me and from what I have
myself partly seen, something of this sort
might be shown her.'

A very curious expression came into
the Viscount's face. He looked at la
Valliere for a few seconds across his wine
in silence. Had la Valliere's plans been
more clearly defined—had he formed, in
fact, any distinct scheme or plan of action
at all—he might have read in the delicate,

worn face much that might have been of use to him, much that might have revealed aspects of human life, of which even he, with all the knowledge of good and evil which his art or craft gave him, was still ignorant.   As it was, however, he noticed merely that there was a somewhat awkward pause.   Then the Viscount said—

'I should think of it, Monsieur, were I you, once or twice.   He is of *la haute noblesse* on the mother's side ; *en outre, elle est si belle.*'

La Valliere looked at his companion with surprise.   Was this the spiteful, gossiping, frivolous chatterer, at once the amusement and the pest of society ?   At his own table, all through the evening, he had been a different man from what la Valliere had known him elsewhere. It seemed as though his other manner had dropped from him as soon as he had left that *vie de société*, for which possibly it had been alone assumed.

'But I thought, Monsieur le Vicomte,' said la Valliere, 'that you had been so anxious that Madame should *se désennuyer?*'

The Viscount looked at him again for a moment.

'*Que voulez-vous? mon cher Monsieur*,' he said. 'Do you take a passing word so much *au sérieux. Une petite bourgeoise perit-être, mais la haute noblesse! c'est tout autre chose.*'

There was an awkward pause; la Fleur fortunately came in with coffee, and the Viscount changed the subject.

'Your friend, de Brie, did not come to the assembly of nobles,' he said. 'I wish you could have been there; you would have gleaned invaluable hints for your art. Picture to yourself such a collection of antiques. We attended mass, and then dined together with Monsieur l'Intendant. It was the only good meal many of them would have in the year. I would warrant that out of all the nobility of the province, and there are thousands, there are not a dozen who have even a decent income. You would have laughed at the comical assemblage.'

La Valliere was too disconcerted to reply. The Viscount went on—

'I sat next an old Don, Monsieur le Comte de la Roche-Anguie d'Avras. It

must have been the only good dinner he
had had for many a day. I was rather
curious to see on what sort of a Rosin-
ante he would depart—the old mares
and other curiosities of horse-flesh would
have delighted a Calot—so I put myself
in his way as we were breaking up, and,
would you believe it, he marched away
on foot!—three leagues if it were a yard!
—to his ruined *château-métairie*, where
they live from year's end to year's end
on pigeons, fowls, and fish. I know the
place—great ruined towers over alleys of
chestnut trees. He wore a long antique
cloak, perfectly brushed, but darned all
round the edges—no doubt by the fair
hands of Mesdames de la Roche-Anguie
d'Avras. I ventured on a little joke as

he came down, about your friend the Countess—Adam and Eve, you know, and—you know the sort of thing. My old Don drew himself up like a poker, looked as though he would have eaten me. Then he pulled his long gray moustache down into his mouth as though he would have eaten it. Then he said,—

'"When I was a boy, Monsieur le Vicomte"—picture to yourself him, or me either for that matter, a boy! "When I was a boy it was held dangerous to joke about a pretty woman in the presence of gentlemen." Then he strode away into the muddy lanes and into the night.'

The Viscount continued his chatter, evidently with the courteous intention of covering la Valliere's embarrassment at the reception his proposal had met with, but la Valliere was too disconcerted to respond.

Suddenly a terrific disturbance made itself heard through the partly open door.

'What is that noise, la Fleur?' said his master, if such he might be called.

'Only the Fléche family, Monsieur,' replied la Fleur. 'The old man has caught that *vaurien*, the gold-worker, who has been forbidden the house, with his daughter, and he and his sons have been dropping him out of one of the front windows. They are really too noisy. I shall have to dismiss them. They pay well, however.'

The Viscount looked at la Valliere for a moment with a meaning smile upon his thin, lined face, but la Valliere did not speak.

The men finished their wine. Then the Viscount conducted his friend to the great door leading to the street. As they went down the staircase the commotion seemed to have subsided. They neither heard nor saw any one.

As la Fleur opened the door for la Valliere to pass out, the Viscount followed him a step into the street—

'Monsieur,' he whispered, taking him by the arm, 'don't do it. Think about it, anticipate it, but don't do it. *Ma foi!* nothing irritates Satan more than that!'

Then he tripped back again into the house, and the great door was closed upon la Valliere and upon the gloomy street.

XI

WHEN la Valliere awoke from a restless, unrefreshing sleep, and remembered the events of the past night and his strange appointment with the Countess Eve, his sensations were of a very conflicting character.

Sprung as he was from a race of born actors, advancing from generation to generation in the social scale and in intellectual acuteness, but not at all in any moral or mental strength, he was himself at last as little under the domain or ordinance of moral responsibility as it is possible for any human creature to be.

The romantic incidents of the last few days, the beauty of the Countess and of her home, the wild, mysterious surroundings of adventure and of intrigue, had impressed his fancy and excited his imagination as an attractive and fantastic play would have done. When he had stood in Paradise the morning before, so far as he was acting for himself at all, and was not the mere instrument of the powers of evil which had gathered round him and found him a compliant and finished tool, his chief idea had been to gratify his desire of having so glorious a creature as the Countess in his own power and possession, to do with her as he would.

He could, however, never properly be said to have any will of his own, for,

according to his training and his creed
of life, it was only the passing fancy of
the moment, the accident of environment,
that attracted his attention or interest,
that was worthy of regard. He had
therefore been greatly impressed by the
way in which his proposal had been
received by the Viscount, and had it
been necessary to take action immediately
on leaving his host, he would probably
have relinquished his intention, though
such conduct would have involved the
breaking of an assignation. But when
he awoke in the morning his first thought
was that the Countess would come out to
meet him in the wood, that he would lift her
upon her horse ; whither he would take her
he knew not. A strange, unusual power

within him—a strength of purpose and of will—surprised even himself. The delight and zest of such an enterprise were pictured to his imagination with a distinctness such as he had never known before.

. In one respect fortune favoured him. There was arranged to be given that afternoon, at a château some leagues from the city, a performance of private theatricals, —*Parade* as it was called, at which all the fashion of the neighbourhood would be present. These *Parades*, which were slight comedies representing the humours of the lower classes, were extremely popular among the aristocracy of the time, and were a sign of the general depravity of taste. The Count, trained in an earlier and severer school of society, detested them.

'It was astonishing to him,' he would say, 'how ladies of standing in society, often of rank and fashion, should condescend to utter sentiments couched in the language of the fishmarket.'

The Count and Countess, therefore, had declined the invitation to be present, but all the rest of the world had accepted, and the neighbourhood of the château of the Countess Eve would in consequence be deserted during the whole of the day.

It seemed indeed as if the powers of evil were allowed a clear field for their malefic work. De Brie, who alone exerted any continuously steadying influence upon his friend, was mysteriously absent,—la Valliere did not know where.

Left to his own devices, as it seemed,
he became an easy prey to those impulses
which he had made the rulers of his life.
He had ordered horses to be ready for
him in the city—one accoutred for a lady;
and accompanied by a boy, he mounted
and rode out at the appointed time.

But as he rode out, his mind was not at
ease. It was one thing to stand in the
radiant garden, in the warm, inspiring sunshine, face to face with perhaps the
loveliest eyes he had ever seen, inspired
too by some strange power which did not
seem his own, and quite another, in the
cool, unexciting, morning hour, to ride out
slowly to an enterprise the end of which he
could not see. The manner in which the
Viscount had received his proposal shewed

him, with distinct clearness, the audacity of his enterprise. Its possible consequences occurred to him with alarming insistence; and as he rode along another difficulty hitherto unthought of perplexed him.

He had intended to leave his horses at the little farm in the valley, where, as we have seen, he had been in the habit of leaving his horse on his visits to the Countess. He had thought that he would then, as usual, have gone on foot to the postern door, and that he would be there at the appointed moment to receive the Countess as she came out. If he had carried out this plan it is possible that the enduring fate of the personages of this story would have been, for every one of them, other than it was.

But a weak, highly-sensitive, and ima-
ginative nature suggested to him end-
less complications. It suddenly occurred
to him, as he rode along, that the people
at the farm had more than once shown
considerable suspicion of his purposes, and
that, should he bring the Countess down
to them, even though she might be
masqued, something unpleasant might be
expected to happen. He was not a
coward, but he was a man of highly-
wrought nervous temperament and susceptibility, and he shrank instinctively
from anything like a scene or contention.

The relations between the *noblesse* and
the peasantry were in those days doubtless
not of the most friendly character, but the
immediate retainers of the nobility were

generally attached to them by interest if
not by affection; and the Count, who had
been long abroad, and had resided for
some years in England, had lost, if he ever
had them, those cruel, insolent feelings with
regard to the peasantry of which some of
the French nobles were accused. He was
respected, and to a certain extent beloved,
by his servants and retainers. Anything
prejudicial to his interests and honour was
certain to be resented by them.

These reflections caused la Valliere to
hesitate. The more he thought of his
scheme, the more wild and dangerous did
it appear. The peculiar susceptibility of
impression which made him a pliant tool in
the hands of evil, at the same time militated
against the absolute dominion of any par-

ticular form of evil. In the sunny garden the morning before, when only the misty outline of his scheme lay before him, it had seemed easy and delicious; now he was more than half inclined to turn back and renounce the whole.

But a complex feeling, made up of vanity and honour, prevented this action. Having pledged his word to be at the garden gate at a certain hour, surely he would keep his tryst; and as he rode along, a mocking, sneering voice seemed ever constant at his ear, insinuating to his fancy the intolerable ignominy that would await a man who, having such a prize within his grasp, faltered from irresolution or from fear, and turned back at the moment of success.

Perplexed by these contradictory emotions, he adopted a timid policy which, as is usually the case, was fatal to the success of his purpose.   He avoided the cottage in the wood, and leaving his horses with the boy in the main road, he determined to await the coming of the Countess at a turn of the wooded path which commanded at once the farmhouse and the horses which he had left. His oscillation and alteration of plan had occasioned some delay, and he did not reach the turn of the path until some moments after that the Countess, true to her time to a second, had opened the postern door ; no finite understanding can realise to the full what the delay of these few seconds meant.

From the point where la Valliere stood he could not see the door.   He waited for a few minutes impatiently, half hoping that she would not come. Then, his anxiety overcoming his prudence, he gave up the sight of the cottage and of his horses, and advanced towards the garden through the shaded pathways of the wood.

It was now near upon midday. The full morning light, the brilliant sunshine, the soft verdure of the green turf and of the fresh leaves, and the dazzling white blossom of the wild cherry trees were all unheeded by him, for before him, as he ascended the path, the postern door stood wide open! the bright light from the outside shining through into the bosky apple groves of Paradise within. There was no trace or sign of the Countess anywhere. What terrible thing had happened? What was the meaning of the open door?

An appalling sense of mystery, a wild
horror and terror such as he had never felt
before, seized upon la Valliere's mind. It
seemed to him that he was conscious
above and around him—in the sunny still
air, in the warmth and glow of life, and of
fresh spring birth — of the presence of
malefic existence, baffled and excited to
despair. The very air he breathed seemed
charged with this environing, oppressive
power and force, terrible from its invisi-
bility. The peculiar faculty with which
he was gifted rose in opposition to this
unseen, intangible oppression and tyranny.
Anything, however appalling to sight and
sense, must be better than this! By a
tremendous effort he concentrated his will,
as he had done before, in a determined

effort to see, and before him, issuing as it were from the open door of Paradise, the Abbé once more stood in his path.

He wished, or so la Valliere's scared fancy showed him, to avoid his recognition, and he seemed to hold the sleeve of his cassock across his face; but la Valliere, maddened with passion and terror, threw himself across his steps.

'Devil! fiend!' he cried; 'where is she? What have you done with her?'

The figure drew the concealing drapery from across its face, and la Valliere staggered backwards, blasted at the sight, so deadly in hate, so vindictive in disappointment and despair, was the expression on the ghastly face he saw.

If there be an annihilation terrible to

the damned, to the lost and utterly malefic being,—an extinction of the evil existence which is its. life and hope, its sole purpose and aim, and which comes to such a being therefore with an intolerable, burning despair — a crouching, craven fear, which spends its last moments in a mad, purposeless, reckless scattering of the venom which was its life,—then such a paroxysm of despairing death, such a final effort of defeated devilry, lashed as with stripes of burning steel across la Valliere's gaze.

'Fool!'—the words hissed upon his face like withering flame—'miserable fool! Go on!'

Unconscious of will or of motion, la Valliere passed through the open door into the blessed sunshine of the garden beyond. Some half-way across the daisied sward, and beneath the apple trees, now laden with a wealth of opening blossom, the Countess Eve, clinging to her husband's arm, was standing in the dazzling light. Beside them, her eyes fixed upon the open door, stood the Abbess; and de Brie, with outstretched hand, stepped forward to meet his friend. Above them, on the distant terrace, beyond the leafy arcades of the garden, the tapering spire of the Tree of Life pointed towards the cloudless sky.

Dazed and confounded as he was by what had passed, scared and distracted by the terrible vision he had just escaped from, la Valliere's eyes were riveted upon another sight—a sight which he was never to forget. He lived to see the massacres of September, and the butchery of the Swiss Guard, yet the sight that haunted him to his deathbed was not these, nor yet that terrible face outside the gate of Paradise, but the Countess's face as she stood clinging to her husband's arm.

Often in the dead of night, after long years had passed away, he would wake up with that lovely face shining out upon him from the darkness, distinct and clear as on that wonderful morn, a radiance of the wondering joy of escape and deliverance upon her lips and within her eyes; but through the meshes of her chestnut hair, and across the gleam of her violet eyes, an appalling mystic light—the singe and glow of the flame of the pit!

The Abbess stood like the archangel of God, the crucifix, that turned its flashing light every way, in her uplifted hand.

'Fear not,' she said, as la Valliere reached his friend; 'he will return no more. The sin which gave him birth, which kept him in existence, and gave him his malefic power, is abolished and blotted out; for by this sign—the sign of the Crucifix—than which none other shall be given while the world endures, Death and Hell are cast into the lake that burns for ever.'

THE END

NEW NOVELS.

THE NEW ANTIGONE. A Romance. 12mo, $1.50.

"The story is marked by great power and an excellent style. . . . Full of questionings which go to the heart of modern science, ethics, and government. . . . The style is mature. the thought cultured. there is an epigrammatic flavor in much of the description which indicates the man of the world."—*New York Tribune.*

"No one who reads the first chapter of 'The New Antigone' can doubt that the author has the rare gift of expressing in the most exquisite language the scenes he imagines so vividly. . . . The book is very far removed from the plane of ordinary novels, and, if a first attempt, is full of promise."—*Guardian.*

FOUR GHOST STORIES. By Mrs. MOLESWORTH, 12mo, $1.50.

"The stories are very well told. There is enough of the uncanny about them to give a pleasant thrill to the reader's nerves. while the supernatural element is not so overdone as to make its unreality palpable."—*Scottish Leader.*

THE NEW JUDGMENT OF PARIS. A Novel. By PHILIP LAFARGUE. 12mo, $1.00.

HARMONIA. A Chronicle. By the author of "Estelle Russell." 12mo, $1.50.

"A curious but decidedly clever story. . . . The scene is laid in Georgia, and the narrative is so full of detail of a peculiar kind that the presumption is strong in favor of a foundation on fact. . . . Altogether 'Harmonia' will be pronounced a successful experiment in such a virgin field."—*New York Tribune.*

"There are several love stories included in the Chronicle, the best of all being that of the young married pair, who stand in the foreground of the tale. In a quiet and leisurely way the book is decidedly interesting and wholesome."—*Christian Union.*

Mrs. PENICOTT'S LODGER, and other Stories. By Lady SOPHIA PALMER. 12mo, $1.00.

"The stories are fresh, compact, vivid. and tender, and written. excepting an occasional obscure sentence, in the facile style which is second nature to our English sisters. and with a directness not always theirs. If the tales cannot be ranked in the first class, they take a highly honorable place in the second."—*Nation.*

ISMAY'S CHILDREN. By the author of "Hogan, M.P.," "Flitters, Tatters, and the Counsellor," etc. 12mo, paper, 50 cents; cloth, $1.00.

"She has written the best novel we have read for years—of its kind. we mean—with a truth which rivals that of Miss Edgeworth's Irish Stories, as well as those of Carleton and the O'Hara Brothers, and with a literary grace and charm which theirs do not possess."—*Mail and Express.*

FOR GOD AND GOLD. By JULIAN CORBETT, author of "The Fall of Asgard." 12mo, $1.50.

"Within its limitations it is not unworthy of being compared with that memorable novel of the Elizabethan age, 'Westward Ho.' . . . From what we have said it will be inferred that this is no ordinary boys' book. but a romance that shows reading, thought, and power in every page."—*Academy.*

"The story is told with excellent force and freshness. The various threads of lines of interest, that of character. that of adventure. that of religious effort and belief, are all so deftly interwoven that it is hard to say to which the story owes its greatest charm."—*Scotsman.*

MACMILLAN & CO., NEW YORK.

MACMILLAN'S POPULAR NOVELS.

Bound in Cloth.

One Dollar Each

By MRS. OLIPHANT.

A COUNTRY GENTLEMAN AND HIS FAMILY.
HESTER.
THE WIZARD'S SON.
SIR TOM.
HE THAT WILL NOT WHEN HE MAY.
YOUNG MUSGRAVE.
THE CURATE IN CHARGE.

By J. H. SHORTHOUSE.

JOHN INGLESANT.
A TEACHER OF THE VIOLIN, Etc.
SIR PERCIVAL.
THE COUNTESS EVE.

By CHARLES KINGSLEY.

WESTWARD HO!
HEREWARD THE WAKE.
TWO YEARS AGO.
ALTON LOCKE, with Portrait.
HYPATIA.
YEAST.

A GREAT TREASON. By MARY A. HOPPUS. 2 vols. $2.50.
MISS BRETHERTON. By Mrs. HUMPHRY WARD. $1.50.
THE MIZ MAZE: A Story. By Nine Authors.
AUNT RACHEL: A Rustic Sentimental Comedy. By J. D. CHRISTIE MURRAY.
CHARLEY KINGSTON'S AUNT. By PEN OLIVER.
JILL. By E. A. DILLWYN.
A DOUBTING HEART. By ANNIE KEARY.
JANET'S HOME. By ANNIE KEARY.
CLEMENCY FRANKLYN. By ANNIE KEARY.

One Dollar and a Quarter Each.

ROBERT ELSMERE. By Mrs. HUMPHRY WARD.
THE REVERBERATOR. By HENRY JAMES.

By CHARLOTTE M. YONGE.

THE HEIR OF REDCLYFFE.
HEARTSEASE.
HOPES AND FEARS.
DYNEVOR TERRACE.
THE DAISY CHAIN.
THE TRIAL.
PILLARS OF THE HOUSE. 2 vols.
CLEVER WOMAN OF THE FAMILY.
THE YOUNG STEPMOTHER.
THE THREE BRIDES.
MY YOUNG ALCIDES.
THE CAGED LION.
THE DOVE IN THE EAGLE'S NEST
THE CHAPLET OF PEARLS.
LADY HESTER AND THE DANVERS PAPERS.
MAGNUM BONUM.
LOVE AND LIFE.
UNKNOWN TO HISTORY.
STRAY PEARLS.
THE ARMOURER'S 'PRENTICES.
THE TWO SIDES OF THE SHIELD.
NUTTIE'S FATHER.
CHANTRY HOUSE

One Dollar and a Half Each.

By F. MARION CRAWFORD.

MR. ISAACS.
ZOROASTER.
SARACINESCA.
DR CLAUDIUS.
A TALE OF A LONELY PARISH.
MARZIO'S CRUCIFIX.

By HENRY JAMES.

THE PRINCESS CASAMASSIMA, $1.75.
THE REVERBERATOR, $1.25.
THE BOSTONIANS, $1.75.
THE ASPERN PAPERS, and other Stories, $1.50.

MACMILLAN & CO., NEW YORK.

MATTHEW ARNOLD'S WORKS.

PUBLISHED BY

MACMILLAN & CO.

PROSE WRITINGS.

LIBRARY EDITION.

In Nine Volumes. Globe 8vo, each, $1.50.

(Uniform with the Eversley Edition of Charles Kingsley's Novels.

CONTENTS OF THE VOLUMES:

Vol. 1. Essays in Criticism.
Vol. 2. On the Study of Celtic Literature — On Translating Homer.
Vol. 3. Culture and Anarchy— Friendship's Garland.
Vol. 4. Mixed Essays—Irish Essays.
Vol. 5. Literature and Dogma.

Vol. 6. God and the Bible.
Vol. 7. St. Paul and Protestantism— Last Essays on Church and Religion.
Vol. 8. Discourses in America.
Vol. 9. Essays in Criticism, Second Series.

The Set of Nine Volumes, in paper box, $13.50.

POEMS.

LIBRARY EDITION.

In Two Volumes. Globe 8vo, $3.50.

Vol. 1. Early Poems, Narrative Poems, and Sonnets.
Vol. 2. Lyric, Dramatic, and Elegiac Poems.

The Prose and Poetical Works, Library Edition, complete in Eleven Volumes, in paper box, $17.00.

American Edition of the Poems, complete in One Volume, 12mo, $1.50.

" It is to him and Clough that the men of the future will come who desire to find the clearest poetic expression of the sentiment and reflection of the most cultivated and thoughtful men of our generation."—*The Nation.*

"Yet I know numbers of young men—and some, alas! no longer young— who have found in Matthew Arnold's poetry a more exact answer to their intellectual and emotional wants than in any poetry of Tennyson's, or even of Emerson's."—*Henry A. Beers, in the Century Magazine.*

"Contains some of the wisest and most melodious verse that this age has produced."—*London Athenæum.*

SELECTED POEMS.

Golden Treasury Series. 18mo, $1.25.

"A volume which is a thing of beauty in itself."—*Pall Mall Gazette.*

PASSAGES FROM THE
PROSE WRITINGS.

12mo, $1.

" Mr. Arnold's writings so abound in impressive and suggestive passages, which bear separation from the text in which they appear, and are worthy of frequent re-reading, that his works may be said to lend themselves in a peculiar and unusual degree to this sort of anthological treatment."
—*Evening Post.*

MACMILLAN & CO.,   NEW YORK.

THE
JOURNAL INTIME

OF

HENRI-FRÉDÉRIC AMIEL.

Translated, with an Introduction and Notes, by

MRS. HUMPHRY WARD.

Crown 8vo, cloth, - - - $2.50.

MACMILLAN & CO., LONDON AND NEW YORK.

Price, in Paper, 50 cents; in Cloth, $1.00.

THE
CHOICE OF BOOKS,
And Other Literary Pieces.

BY

FREDERIC HARRISON.

FROM THE NATION.

"This study of a man (St. Bernard de Morlaix) who repre-sents almost, if not quite, ideally the typical Apostle of Humanity, in whom mere excellence dominates and blesses the life of men in their grand social relations, is the most valuable of the fifteen papers which the book contains, and is of the highest moral reach and sug-gestiveness. The same seriousness, though not so intense, pervades the book ; and though there are many passages of cleverness, of wit and sharp sarcasm, and flashes of the lighter play of his brilliant literary art, the preacher's earnestness is never far away. It is good sermonizing, too. The glowing indignation at the lot of the poor, the fixed faith in the destiny of the people, the unrestrained denun-ciation of the waste and folly of the energies and pursuits of most of us, kindle many an ardent page ; and through all breathes the spirit of a man who, whether duped or inspired, is settled on doing his part in the work of the time. To read such words is both vivifying and humanizing. There is instruction to be had also. "The Choice of Books" is the sage advice of so many wise men repeated once more—to trust the sentence of the race and read the classics. The essay on Carlyle is at once appreciative of his genius and character and just to his stupendous errors. The paper on the eighteenth cen-tury, with its widening of the field of view, and the one on the nine-teenth, with its interrogations as to the justice of our self-gratulation, are admirable examples of the way in which historical periods should be examined ; and these, which we have mentioned, are typical of the whole contents of a volume which, though it belongs to magazine literature, attains the highest level in that class."

MACMILLAN & CO., NEW YORK.

COMPLETE IN FOUR VOLUMES.

Student's Edition, in box, $4.00 : Each Vol. $1.09.
Cabinet   "   " $5.00: Sold in sets only.

THE ENGLISH POETS.

SELECTIONS,

With Critical Introductions by Various Writers,
and a General Introduction by
MATTHEW ARNOLD.

EDITED BY THOMAS HUMPHRY WARD, M.A.

Vol. I.—CHAUCER TO DONNE.
Vol. II.—BEN JONSON TO DRYDEN.
Vol. III.—ADDISON TO BLAKE.
Vol. IV.—WORDSWORTH TO ROSSETTI.

MACMILLAN & CO., NEW YORK.

MACMILLAN'S

GLOBE LIBRARY.

The editors, by their scholarship and special study of these authors, are competent to afford every assistance to readers of all kinds. This assistance is rendered by original biographies, glos-saries of unusual or obsolete words, and critical and explanatory notes.

SHAKESPEARE. Edited by W. G. CLARK, M. A., and W. ALDIS WRIGHT, M. A.

" For the busy man, above all for the working student, this is the best of all existing Shakespeares." — *Athenæum.*

SPENSER. Edited by RICHARD MORRIS.

SCOTT. Edited by FRANCIS TURNER PALGRAVE.

BURNS. Edited by ALEXANDER SMITH.

" The most interesting edition which has ever been published." — *Bell's Life.*

GOLDSMITH. Edited by PROFESSOR MASSON.

POPE. Edited by A. W. WARD.

DRYDEN. Edited by W. D. CHRISTIE.

" An admirable edition." — *Pall Mall Gazette.*

COWPER. Edited by REV. W. BENHAM.

MORTE D'ARTHUR. CAXTON'S EDITION, revised for modern use.

ROBINSON CRUSOE. From the Original Editions. Ed-ited by HENRY KINGSLEY.

" A book to *have* and to *keep.*" — *Star.*

VIRGIL. Rendered into English Prose by LONSDALE and LEE.

" A more complete edition of Virgil in English it is scarcely possible to con-ceive than the scholarly work before us." — *Globe.*

HORACE. By the same translators.

MILTON. Edited by PROFESSOR MASSON.

Each volume in cloth, $1.25; or in half calf, library style, $2.25.

" A series yet unrivaled for its combination of excellence and cheapness." — *Daily Telegraph.*

MACMILLAN & CO., New York.